THE CANNIBAL
WHO OVERATE

THE CANNIBAL
WHO OVERATE

Hugh Pentecost

DODD, MEAD & COMPANY

NEW YORK

Copyright © 1962 by Judson Philips
All rights reserved
No part of this book may be reproduced in any form
without permission in writing from the publisher

Published by Dodd, Mead & Company, Inc.
79 Madison Avenue, New York, N.Y. 10016

Distributed in Canada by
McClelland and Stewart Limited, Toronto

Manufactured in the United States of America

First Red Badge printing

Library of Congress Catalog Card Number: 62-10057
ISBN: 0-396-08237-8

PART 1

IT WAS MONDAY.

The coming Saturday would be the Great Man's birthday. It would be celebrated lavishly but not lovingly. Mr. Pierre Chambrun, resident manager of the Hotel Beaumont, found himself surrounded by tensions he had experienced only once before—the morning of D day at a coastal town in Britain, waiting for Eisenhower to give the final word to "go." Mr. Chambrun had been involved in one other party of the Great Man's, but he had gone into that one with babelike innocence. Mr. Chambrun was one of the very top hotel operators in the business. A party, no matter how elaborate or expensive, was not a cause for tensions in his world. But he had learned. The Great Man had a kind of genius that could turn the sweet simplicity of a child's christening into a complete hell. His particular brand of sadism was so complex that not a single member of the Beaumont's staff nor, in fact, not one of its guests would remain untouched in the next six days.

The Great Man's diabolism would begin at ten o'clock sharp on this Monday morning and would last until early the following Sunday morning when an exhausted crew of waiters, bus boys and porters began to clean up the debris left behind in the Beaumont's ballroom by some two hundred and fifty guests.

While Mr. Pierre Chambrun might feel tensions, he was not nervy or in any sense a coward. He had been a better than good soldier in the war because he wasn't one of those knuckle-headed heroes who rush into danger without any thought of the risks. His vivid imagination could foresee all the dangers, so that the courage involved in facing them was very real. His daily routine as resident manager of the Beaumont covered a variety of situations that called for tact as well as iron nerve. Despite its reputation as the top luxury residence hotel in New York, the Beaumont was confronted with many of the same problems as lesser establishments. There were always the drunks, the dead beats, the call girls—the most expensive in New York but nonetheless call girls—the endless cantankerous and baseless complaints, the suicides, the heart attacks suffered by elderly gentlemen, the whims of elderly dowagers with so much money they couldn't have told you how much it was, the oddities, like the Greek gentleman on the twenty-fourth floor who had been happily whipping two girls tied to his bedposts and would have got away with it if he hadn't tried to add an innocent chambermaid to his collection of masochists. Mr. Chambrun handled these and many other problems with suave efficiency. But a party by the Great Man—!

At the Beaumont you give extra care and attention, not to pleasant dispositions who are generous with their gratuities, but to dollar signs. The Great Man had paid $194,000 for his eight-room cooperative apartment and the annual maintenance fee was $32,000. For this the Beaumont and its staff took its own particular kind of beating. You said "sir" to the Great Man even though your thoughts were far from respectful.

Mr. Chambrun, aware of what this week held for him and his staff, lit an Egyptian cigarette and looked out his broad office window facing Central Park. He was a small, dark man, stocky in build, with heavy pouches under dark eyes that could be hard as a hanging judge's or unexpectedly twinkle with humor. He was, as his name suggests, French by birth, but he had come to this country as a small boy and he thought like an American. His training in the hotel business had taken him back to Europe; he spoke several languages fluently; he could adopt a Continental manner to suit an occasion; but he thought like an American.

"Jerk," he said to the green acres of Central Park.

There were two sensitive areas that needed alerting. Mr. Chambrun swung around in his swivel chair and picked up one of the several phones on his desk.

"Yes, please?"

"Mr. Chambrun here, Jane. May I speak to Mrs. Veach?"

"Right away, sir."

Mr. Chambrun smiled faintly. In the old days the switchboard operators had answered the phone with the phrase, "May I help you?" The results hadn't always been pleasant. "How about popping up to room 2404—if you're blonde and built?" "Yes, please," was much safer.

Mrs. Veach, the chief operator, was a large, bosomy, motherly woman. She took great pride in the efficiency, tact and down-to-earth sophistication of her girls. With an estimated eighty percent of the male residents of the hotel cheating on their women, the handling of incoming calls and messages required a cynical awareness of the in's and out's of hundreds of private lives.

"Good morning, Mr. Chambrun," Mrs. Veach said in her best headmistress manner.

"Lovely morning."

"Yes, Mr. Chambrun."

"To become less lovely."

"I trust there are no complaints, Mr. Chambrun. My

9

records show we handled eleven hundred calls yesterday without an error."

"Your record will not be as good today. Are you sitting down, Mrs. Veach?"

"I beg your pardon?"

"Are you sitting down?"

"Yes, sir."

"The Great Man is giving a birthday party on Saturday night. The wheels will begin to turn at ten o'clock. I suggest you assign one girl to handle all the calls from Penthouse M, in and out, and all Mr. Amato's calls."

"Saturday night!" Mrs. Veach said, her voice cracking.

"Not much time for that kind of brawl, Mrs. Veach. The wires will hum. Do your best."

"That's what I'm here for, Mr. Chambrun."

"Of course. And you always do. Now will you have me connected with Mr. Amato?"

"At once, Mr. Chambrun."

Mr. Chambrun put out his cigarette in the brass ashtray on his desk. He did it slowly and thoughtfully.

"Banquet Manager!" said a buoyant, cheerful voice.

"Amato? Chambrun here."

"Good morning, Mr. Chambrun. Beautiful day."

"Perhaps. I find a memo on my desk, Amato, from the Great Man in Penthouse M. He has decided to give a birthday party for himself in the ballroom on Saturday night for two hundred and fifty guests."

"*This* Saturday?"

"This Saturday."

"Oh, God!"

"Precisely."

"Oh, God!"

"Now I am on my way to your office, Amato, to hold your hand for a few moments before you go up for an audience with His Majesty at ten o'clock."

"Oh, God!"

"I'm on my way, Amato. Be good enough to take your Bromo Seltzer and your nerve medicine before I get there. I find that watching you gulp down your pharmaceuticals at nine thirty in the morning has a tendency to make me feel sympathetically distressed."

"Oh, God!" Mr. Amato said in a faraway voice.

Mr. Chambrun took the elevator from his fourth floor office down to the Beaumont's lobby. His practiced eye took in the details of the lobby in an almost subconscious check. All well at the newsstand. The lighted display of jewels in the window of Tiffany's branch office had been changed since yesterday and was eye-catching. Winter ski clothes had replaced the evening dresses in Bonwit's window. Jerry Dodd, the house officer, standing near the first bank of elevators, nodded cheerfully. "House dick" was a phrase that wouldn't have been permitted at the Beaumont.

Mr. Chambrun stopped at the desk. Mr. Atterbury, the reservations clerk, greeted him with a relaxed smile. "Everything taken except the house seats," he reported.

The "house seats" were two suites held in reserve by the management to cover the unexpected arrival of important guests. Only Mr. Chambrun and the owner, Mr. George Battle, could approve their use. Since Mr. Battle lived permanently on the French Riviera, presumably counting his money and never coming to the end of the count, Mr. Chambrun really controlled the "house seats."

"No fireworks during the night?" Mr. Chambrun asked.

"Nothing on the night score-card," Mr. Atterbury said.

Mr. Chambrun turned away, intending to walk directly to the far end of the lobby and Mr. Amato's office. Just as he turned, the doors to one of the express elevators opened and something like an apparition appeared.

The "apparition" was an old, very erect, very grand lady. Her mink coat was of an antiquated cut, but the furs were magnificent. A matching muff was hung around her neck by a black cord. Her left hand was buried in the muff. Her right hand held a dog leash. On the end of the leash was a small, black-and-white Japanese spaniel, wheezing a bit through its snub nose. Mr. Chambrun moved toward the old lady, remembering that Mrs. George Haven was referred to by the staff as "the Madwoman of Chaillot." She might be mad, but she owned the second most expensive apartment in the Beaumont.

Mr. Chambrun gave Mrs. Haven his best heel-clicking bow and the number-one smile. "Good morning, Mrs. Haven," he said. "Beautiful morning."

The spaniel gave Mr. Chambrun a hostile look. The lady gave him no look at all. He might not have been there. He suspected that if he hadn't stepped back she would have rolled over him with the grim precision of an army tank. He watched her go out through the revolving doors onto Fifth Avenue, the spaniel waddling beside her.

"Still getting the brush, Mr. Chambrun?" Jerry Dodd asked at the manager's elbow.

Mr. Chambrun permitted himself a rueful smile. "Seven months, Jerry," he said. "Mrs. Haven has been with us for seven months. Each day of those seven months I have said good morning to her and each day of those seven months she has passed me by as though I was an armchair against the wall. There have been no complaints, no problems, but in some fashion I have offended her. It haunts me, Jerry."

"Maybe you're just lucky," the house officer said. "She talks to Waters, the doorman, by the hour. He looks pretty pooped when she gets through with him."

12

"It's not conversation I want, Jerry. But my curiosity is piqued. What have I done to offend her?"

"Maybe you should let it lay," Jerry said. "You might be opening up a can of peas."

"That could be sage advice, my friend."

The froth of a hastily gulped Bromo Seltzer rimmed the water glass on Mr. Amato's desk. On a table beside the desk was a collection of medicines—pills, liquids, powders—that looked recently disturbed. Mr. Amato was a tall, dark, thin, and at the moment, very pale man in his early forties. He was a Roman, and he must have been a very beautiful young man with a profile like a god on a coin. There were now little puffs, and pouches, and lines that suggested dyspepsia and incipient ulcers. As Mr. Chambrun came into the office Mr. Amato was wringing his hands like a bereaved mother at a battlefield grave.

"If I were to quit right now, without notice, what would you do?" Mr. Amato asked.

"Try to hire the banquet manager away from the Hotel Pierre," Mr. Chambrun said placidly. He sat down beside Mr. Amato's desk and lit one of his Egyptian cigarettes.

"How can I buy beef that's been properly aged for two hundred and fifty people?" Mr. Amato wailed. "You can't buy aged beef in quantity on such short notice."

"Let 'em eat cake," Mr. Chambrun said, smiling.

"Do you know what this means?" Mr. Amato cried. "Argument on every item of food, on every bottle of wine, on every detail of service. And when it's exactly as he orders it, he will complain that it isn't exactly as he ordered it. My best captains will threaten to leave unless the bribe is very high."

"A bribe which His Majesty will pay," Mr. Chambrun said, unmoved.

"I know from the last time! Flowers will have to be flown from Hawaii; special salmon from the Canadian Northwest; wines that are not in our cellar—"

"There are no such wines," Mr. Chambrun said.

"What madness will have seized him this time?"

"My advice to you is to throw him a curve or two."

"Curve?"

"Beat him to the draw, as they say on the TV."

"How?"

Mr. Chambrun smoothed his little black mustache with an immaculate forefinger. "Kangaroo tail soup," he said. "With it, by the way, you serve a Madeira, Special."

"Kangaroo tail soup!"

Mr. Chambrun smiled dreamily. "Specially flown in from Australia."

"Is it good?" Mr. Amato asked, practicality taking hold.

"It is unbelievably foul-tasting," Mr. Chambrun said, happily. "But the two hundred and fifty guests will eat every last drop of it lest somebody should guess that they have no palate at all. It should give you a moment of exquisite pleasure in a time of tribulation, Amato."

A comically sinister smile flickered on Mr. Amato's pale lips. "Kangaroo tail soup!" he said, softly. "Thank you, Mr. Chambrun."

"Any time." Mr. Chambrun put out his cigarette. "I recognize the aged beef as a problem. I suggest you try to sell his nibs on Roast Venison Gran Veneur. With it, artichoke bottoms with purée of chestnuts."

"You wouldn't need to hire Rama if I quit," Mr. Amato said.

"Just settle down to your job, Amato. His Majesty can't kill you. A week from today will be another Monday and it will all be behind you." Mr. Chambrun glanced at the wall clock behind Mr. Amato's desk. It showed five minutes to ten. "I suggest one more Bromo Seltzer, and then into the breach, dear friend."

Mrs. Veach, the chief operator, had moved promptly and efficiently. At five minutes to ten, circuits had been shifted. Jane Prindle, a snub-nosed redhead and her best operator, had been set to handle the board which would take only calls from and for Penthouse M and for Mr. Amato, who would presently be calling to all points on this man's earth.

A red light flashed on from Penthouse M.

"Here we go," Jane said, in a dry voice. Then, sweetly, as she made the connection, "Yes, please?"

A cold, thin voice with a strongly British intonation came over the wire. "The correct time, please."

Jane deftly broke the connection. "His Majesty is giving a million dollar party but he's too cheap to buy a clock." The connection was remade. "One minute past ten," Jane said, again all sweetness and light.

"You are certain?"

"Yes, sir. Western Union clock."

"Thank you."

The connection was broken. "Well, now he knows what time it is," Jane said.

"Connect me with Mr. Amato," Mrs. Veach said to the operator sitting next to Jane.

Mr. Amato, less than normally cheerful, answered the call.

"Mrs. Veach here, Mr. Amato," the chief operator said. "His Majesty has just called down to check on the time. You are already one minute and thirty-four seconds late for your appointment with him."

"Oh, God!" Mr. Amato said.

15

TWO

When a man reaches the venerable age of seventy-five it seems perfectly logical that his birthday should be celebrated. When he is a famous man, known the world over, honored in his profession for more than fifty years, one might expect notables from all over the world to make the effort to be present at the party.

You might expect the party to be given for him by his admirers. Even though the birthday boy happened to be one of the richest men in the world, you'd still expect him to be honored by others.

But the projected party which had already thrown the staff of the Hotel Beaumont into a dither was being given by the Great Man himself. The guest list would be surprising because of the absence of other great names. Aubrey Moon's seventy-fifth birthday would be peopled by a strange assortment of punks, chiselers, neurotics, alcoholics, nymphos, and cheap adventurers. There would be a few honest members of the press, a few odd political figures, and a handful of highly respectable people who shouldn't have allowed themselves to be caught dead at Aubrey Moon's party.

Aubrey Moon!

British by birth, Moon came into a large fortune at the age of twenty-one. That would have been in 1908. His first stories were effete and obscure, published in little art magazines on the left bank of the Seine. He was a lavish party giver, even in those days. And even in those days it was notable that real friends quickly peeled away from him like the skin off a banana. His chief delight in life, then and now, was finding the weak spots in people and exposing them without pity, cruelly. He was to be avoided like a poison jellyfish. In those early days he dealt in little infidelities—the exposure of which resulted in broken homes; in moral oddities, equally destructive; in other people's desperate dishonesties. Later on, when his obscure style had been tossed aside by the influence of such master storytellers as Kipling and Somerset Maugham, he became a top war correspondent. His cruelties and his reputation grew now, for he revealed the secrets of people in high places. It was an insatiable thirst for power and the ability to control the lives of important men and women. All in the name of honest, crusading journalism. He was feared and hated—and accepted, because to snub or ignore him was to suggest to the world that you had something to fear. After the war, came world travel, novels and plays, a Pulitzer Prize and eventually the Nobel Prize for Literature. Hollywood poured gold into his already overstuffed bank accounts. He could build a little actress or a little actor to stardom. But watch out! His hands were on the props and he could—and would—pull them out at a chosen moment and send reputations and careers crashing to earth. Moon had stuck his fingers into many pies that were neither British nor American. He had been an inveterate world traveler after World War I. He knew the Middle East like few English-speaking men of his time. He had climbed mountains. He had flown planes. He had—he announced at regular intervals—made love, successfully, to women of all colors.

"I will never forget that little bead-wrestler in Naples," he would say, at one and the same time defiling Italian womanhood and the Catholic Church.

This, on a thumbnail, was Aubrey Moon.

At seventy-five Moon was a caricature of himself at thirty. He had been handsome and romantic in the days of World War I, uniformed, swagger-sticked, jaunty; tall, dark, well boned, with an insolent little black mustache and raven black hair, sleek and shining. At seventy-five his hair and mustache were still black, but

17

obviously not as a result of a special gift of nature. They were expertly dyed. His cheeks were puffy and pale, and there were two great pouches under his eyes. The mouth under the dyed mustache was thin and invariably twisted by a cruel little smile. There was no one too insignificant or too important for him to devour —from a bus boy to a president.

Two years ago Aubrey Moon had come to the Beaumont, bent on purchasing one of the elaborate cooperative apartments—a penthouse. Mr. Chambrun had shown him Penthouse L which was vacant and for sale. Moon was unruffled by the price—$194,000. He may not even have heard the annual maintenance fee of $32,000.

"This is quite satisfactory," he told Mr. Chambrun. "But I want Penthouse M."

"Penthouse M is already owned and occupied, Mr. Moon," Mr. Chambrun told him. "But L is identical with M."

"I want M," Aubrey Moon said. "I will pay the current owner of M ten thousand dollars to make the switch with me."

"Quite impossible. The present owner of M doesn't need ten thousand dollars, Mr. Moon."

"Then the deal is off."

Mr. Chambrun's shrug hid his disappointment. "As you please. But may I ask why you wish Penthouse M?"

"It's quite simple. My name begins with M. I want Penthouse M or I go elsewhere."

Mr. Chambrun's face revealed nothing. "Suppose I could persuade the occupant of Penthouse M to allow me to remove the letter 'M' from the door and replace it with the letter 'L,' thus making it possible for me to screw the letter 'M' to your door. Would that be satisfactory? I should think the labor would come to less than five dollars."

"As long as my apartment is known as Penthouse M—"

That was the beginning of a long chess game between Mr. Chambrun and Aubrey Moon, a game which Mr. Chambrun could play with consummate skill.

It was of no concern to Mr. Chambrun that Aubrey Moon's bed was a replica of an old Chinese junk. It was of no concern to him that Penthouse M was furnished with Burmese screens, Chinese brocades, Tibetan Buddhas, lavish Oriental rugs. It was of no concern to him that the living room was dominated by a kind of reclining throne, its foam-rubber mattress covered with Japanese silks. It did not disturb Mr. Chambrun that on his infrequent visits to the penthouse he found himself looking up at Moon, reclining on his throne, smoking a cigarette through a long jade holder, sipping a glass of iced coconut milk. Mr. Amato would feel like a serf, crawling on his knees. Mr. Chambrun felt contempt for Aubrey Moon, and he could afford to because Moon had absolutely nothing on him. His only problem was to keep from laughing in the presence of the Great Man.

Mr. Chambrun was a rare man in his own right. He was vulnerable in only one area. He was unaware that Moon recognized his temptation to laughter and hated his guts for it. The razor-sharp blade of Aubrey Moon's hostility was waiting patiently for Mr. Chambrun's guard to drop.

Margo Stewart sat at a little portable typewriter table a few feet from the base of Aubrey Moon's living room throne. He had just hung up the phone at his elbow after asking the switchboard for the correct time.

"Mr. Amato will pay for this little discourtesy," Moon said. "I will not have servants treating me in this cavalier fashion. Let's see, Sandy, where were we?"

Margo Stewart's fair hair and her tendency to freckle

in the summer time had earned her the nickname of Sandy many years ago. Only a very few people whom she liked still used it—and Aubrey Moon.

She was forced to look up. Moon lay stretched out on his Japanese silks, the jade cigarette holder between his thin lips, his bright black eyes behind their pouches staring down at her. She had the feeling that from his point of elevation he was looking right down inside the front of her dress. She felt her nerves grow tense. It was like having some sort of loathsome spider crawling over her naked flesh. And sometime, she thought, with a kind of icy horror, it might happen. Sometime when her own special problem had left her unguarded.

She drew a deep breath. "Entertainment," she said. "Will you want Mr. Waldron of the hotel's entertainment department to handle it?"

"I do not want Mr. Waldron of the hotel entertainment department to handle anything for me," Moon said, in his thin, acid voice. "By the way, Sandy, I prefer your V-cut necklines to that square thing. I do not belong to the school which believes that Puritan severity is more titillating than outright revelation. Make a note. V-cut necklines during working hours."

She sat rigidly silent in front of her machine, her hands resting on the space bar to keep them from shaking.

"It always surprises me, Sandy, when I'm reminded of what a little prude you are." A thin little chuckle grated on her nerves. "Well, back to entertainment. You will call the Metropolitan Opera and tell them I want the entire chorus and ensemble of the company here after their Saturday night performance."

The typewriter clicked softly. Sandy had been with Moon long enough not to be surprised. He could very well have asked for the members of the Supreme Court to be present and they'd probably have come.

"Do you have some special music in mind?" she asked.

"As the cake—which I envisage as an architectural triumph—is brought into the ballroom at the end of dinner, they will sing 'Happy Birthday.'"

"But for their main performance?"

"My dear Sandy, that will be their main—and only —performance. They will sing 'Happy Birthday dear Aubrey' and go home."

Even she was staggered. "The Metropolitan Opera Chorus?"

"Can you think of anyone who could sing it better? If you can, we'll have them."

"I can't think of any better choral group."

"Fine. By the way, the hotel will want to take advantage of my party to issue promotion and publicity of their own. I want to be certain it's the kind of publicity I approve. You will ask the Public Relations director to come here for a chat with me at two o'clock. What is her name?"

"Alison Barnwell," Sandy said, her eyes fixed on her typewriter. She could almost feel Moon's sardonic smile.

"What is your judgment of Miss Barnwell, Sandy?"

"I have no judgment, Mr. Moon. She's always been very courteous and friendly."

"I wonder how friendly she could be?" Moon asked, his voice soft and feline. "Long legs, thoroughbred carriage, natural red hair. Full of the juices of living, I should think." He paused. "Well, Sandy?"

"I have no opinion, Mr. Moon."

"Of course you have. You resent her because she is so many things you are not! Well, have her here at two o'clock. And, Sandy—"

"Yes, Mr. Moon."

"You can take a couple of hours off at that time. I won't be needing you."

The doorbell rang.

"That will be Mr. Amato," Sandy said.

"Let him in," Moon said, his thin smile twisted to one side, "and leave him to me! I suggest you go to your cubbyhole and get on to the Opera at once. Their price, you understand, is our price."

Sandy got up and walked to the door. Mr. Amato stood outside, laden down with papers and notebooks, sweating.

"Good morning, Mr. Amato," Sandy said.

"Good morning, Miss Stewart."

"Mr. Moon has been waiting for you."

"I'm sorry to be late. I—"

"This way, Mr. Amato."

Moon, a Japanese kimono draped around his shoulders, stared down at Mr. Amato. The sharp black eyes flickered toward his gold wrist watch.

"I trust, Mr. Amato, you have some explanation for being seven minutes late."

"I was trying to anticipate your needs," Mr. Amato chattered. "I knew you would ask certain questions—I wanted to have the answers for them. I felt certain you would—"

Sandy walked away toward the far door. Her sound-proofed "cubbyhole" lay just beyond it. But she slowed down as she approached the door. Just to the right of it was a teakwood cabinet which was used as a bar. On its flat top were whiskies, gins, scotches, vodkas, brandies.

Vodka, Sandy thought, left almost no odor on your breath. Just one good slug of vodka would save her life. But at seven minutes past ten in the morning?

She moved quickly through the door, closing it behind her. In the cubbyhole she sat down at her desk. The palms of her hands were damp.

She was just reaching for the phone when it gave a soft purring sound. She picked it up.

"Mr. Moon's apartment."

"This is Mr. Gamayel, Miss Stewart." The voice was cultivated, Oxfordian, yet with a faint foreign flavor. Ozman Gamayel was the Egyptian diplomat who had a temporary suite on the eleventh floor of the Beaumont.

"Good morning, Mr. Gamayel."

"I suppose," Mr. Gamayel said, in his precise, studied way, "it is useless to ask you to connect me with Mr. Moon?"

"Quite useless, I'm afraid."

"I could make it very worth your while, Miss Stewart. If you would just put me through I would take my chances."

"I'm sorry, Mr. Gamayel. If I put you through he would hang up immediately and then proceed to fire me."

A long sigh came over the wire. "Do you have any idea when he may be going out?"

"I have no idea, Mr. Gamayel. He may not go out at all—for days. He's planning a birthday party for Saturday night."

"Another birthday party!"

Sandy felt a cold finger run along her spine. The controlled hatred in the soft voice on the other end was frightening. "I can tell you this, Mr. Gamayel. You are on the list of guests to be invited. Perhaps you can talk to him then."

"I am always invited," Mr. Gamayel said, "for the annual pleasure it gives him to spit on me. Please forgive my vulgarity, Miss Stewart."

"Of course."

There was another long pause and then the phone went dead. After a moment Sandy picked up the phone again. Her voice wasn't quite steady.

"Jane? Would you connect me with Miss Barnwell in the Public Relations office?"

Alison Barnwell never sounded tired or done in by the madhouse she worked in. It almost made you feel better to hear the buoyancy in her voice.

"This is Sandy Stewart, Alison."

"Hi, darling. How are you?" Alison said. "I take it we're about to go into orbit."

"Mr. Amato's with my boss now."

"Poor devil," Alison said.

"I'm to ask you to come to the penthouse at two o'clock. Mr. Moon wants to discuss publicity with you."

"I'll bow in on the dot," Alison said.

"Alison?"

"Something wrong, Sandy? You sound queer."

"Just a little beat," Sandy said. "Alison?"

"Yes?"

"Could you send someone else to see him? I mean, you could be ill, or have a fashion show you have to cover, or something."

"My dear child, at the Beaumont we drop everything at a whisper from the Great Man."

"Don't see him, Alison!"

There was a brief silence and then Alison's laugh, warm and unafraid, came over to Sandy. "So the Great Man is in his wolf mood! Cheer up, Sandy. I'm a big girl. Remember?"

THREE

Mr. Pierre Chambrun never ate lunch. As resident manager of the Hotel Beaumont his services were called on most frequently between the hours of eleven and three; people with complaints, people with special problems, members of the staff confronted by one difficulty or another, outside interests using the hotel for parties, fashion shows, special conferences. The arrivals and

24

departures of celebrities, notables, and the just plain rich required special attention. Though there were special departments and department heads for handling the intricacies of travel arrangements, publicity tie-ins and general bowings and scrapings, Mr. Chambrun was always close at hand for the emergencies. He had a gift for delegating authority but he was always ready to take the full responsibility for a touchy decision. He could make such decisions on the instant, and after thirty years in the hotel business he could tell himself without vanity that he had never made a decision he felt later had been an error. A few of them had proved wrong or unworkable, but he knew that faced with the same situation again he would make the same judgment.

Mr. Chambrun always ate a hearty breakfast: fruit juice, lamb chops or a small steak or sometimes brook trout or a Dover sole, toast in quantity with sweet butter and marmalade or jam. And coffee—coffee which he went on drinking all day. At seven in the evening he ate an elaborate dinner designed to meet the requirements of a gourmet's palate.

The staff at the Beaumont had come to understand Mr. Chambrun. He appeared to spend most of his time doing nothing, but actually it was soon apparent that he had some kind of built-in radar system that alerted him to situations almost before they developed.

On that Monday a few minutes before one o'clock Mr. Chambrun was at his desk in the fourth-floor office, sipping his inevitable cup of coffee and smoking an Egyptian cigarette, his heavy lidded eyes watching some children sliding down a snow-covered knoll in Central Park. His secretary announced, over the intercom system, that Mr. Ozman Gamayel was in the outer office wishing to see him. Mr. Chambrun got up from his desk and went to the door to greet his visitor personally.

"A pleasure, Mr. Gamayel," he said. "Do come in. I have some freshly brewed Turkish coffee here if you'd care to join me in a cup."

"I should enjoy it," Mr. Gamayel said.

He sat down in the armchair beside Mr. Chambrun's desk. The Egyptian diplomat was a small man, thin, with a coffee-colored skin and sad, dark brown eyes. He wore a black overcoat with a rich fur collar. He carried a black Malacca walking stick with a heavy silver knob. He wore a carefully brushed derby hat.

"Let me take your coat, sir," Chambrun said. "The temperature in here is exactly seventy degrees. You will be overheated when you go out."

"Thank you."

Gamayel removed his coat, revealing a fur-lined interior. He handed the coat and derby hat to Mr. Chambrun, retaining the Malacca cane. His hair was black, shiny and meticulously combed. He sat down in the armchair.

From a sideboard Mr. Chambrun produced two fresh demitasse-size cups of Turkish coffee. He pushed a cigarette box across the desk to Gamayel's elbow. He sat down in his own chair, eyebrows slightly raised in an expression of polite inquiry.

"It is peaceful here," Gamayel said. He sipped the coffee. "Perfection."

"Thank you, sir. I brew it myself. There are certain things one trusts to no one else."

"Which," Gamayel said, "is why I am here, Mr. Chambrun."

"I am flattered—and at your service."

"I wish to arrange for plane tickets for myself and my secretary to Alexandria for as soon after midnight on Saturday as can be managed."

"A simple matter," Mr. Chambrun said. "Our travel bureau—"

"I do not wish your travel bureau to handle it,"

Gamayel said. "If I had felt it was a routine matter I should not be taking up your valuable time."

"Oh."

"I wish to be able to leave without attracting any attention whatsoever, Mr. Chambrun. I do not wish to announce that I am checking out. I shall leave funds with you to take care of my indebtedness to the hotel after I am gone."

"I see."

"I believe you can arrange reservations for me without using my name. I am a director of the firm of Zaki and Sons, importers of rare perfumes. You can say that some member of the firm must make the trip to Alexandria, but that it will not be decided until the last moment who shall make the trip. Of course my passport and other papers are in order."

"It can be managed."

"I say as soon after midnight as possible," Gamayel said, "but bear in mind that I shall be a guest at Aubrey Moon's birthday party until precisely midnight. I will not be able to leave until the last stroke of twelve has sounded. Thus time must be allowed for me to get to the airport after that. If there is no flight until morning I shall find a way to use up the time, away from the hotel."

"Your luggage?"

"My luggage, my personal belongings, Mr. Chambrun, will be taken out bit by bit during the week so that on Sunday morning, when I leave the party, it will seem I am just going out for a breath of fresh air before turning in—a practice I have carried out for the last three months."

"I should have the reservations for you before the end of the afternoon," Mr. Chambrun said. "I will notify you at once."

"Please do not notify me over the telephone," Gamayel said. "I am well aware of, and compliment you upon, the complete discretion of your telephone staff. Nonetheless, I do not choose to run the slightest risk of my departure being known to anyone but you."

"I'm flattered by your confidence."

The sad dark eyes stared steadily at Mr. Chambrun. "Your curiosity is piqued?"

Mr. Chambrun laughed pleasantly. "If the man in this job allowed his curiosity to gnaw away at him, Mr. Gamayel, he would very soon find himself a patient in an ulcer clinic. You have asked for a discreet service. It will be performed for you." His heavy eyelids lowered. "I admit to a certain curiosity, but it is unrelated to your travel plans."

"Oh?"

"I find myself wondering why a man of your position, distinction and wealth allows himself to become involved in a piece of vulgarity like Aubrey Moon's birthday party. In your position, Mr. Gamayel, I should get my breath of fresh air much earlier in the evening. I happen to know there is a jet flight for Alexandria about eleven o'clock."

A nerve twitched, high up on a coffee-colored cheek. "Your acute powers of observation are a legend among the guests of this hotel, Mr. Chambrun."

"Forgive me if I've been impertinent."

Gamayel stood up. Mr. Chambrun instantly got the coat and derby hat from the rack in the corner. Gamayel leaned on the Malacca stick, his hand white around the silver knob, He took a deep breath, put the cane down on the desk, and allowed Mr. Chambrun to help him into the fur-lined coat. He placed the derby hat carefully on his head. He spoke as if the choice of words was of the utmost importance.

"I asked you about your curiosity and you answered me honestly, Mr. Chambrun. It was not an impertinence. It was, however, very close to what you call in this country, I believe, a bull's-eye. The answer to your question would be far too revealing for comfort. But one of these days you may have it. Thank you for your courtesy, Mr. Chambrun."

"A pleasure to serve you. And I have a piece of advice for you."

Gamayel turned sharply to stare at Mr. Chambrun. The resident manager's eyes twinkled. "If you must go to the Moon party, sir, avoid the kangaroo tail soup like the plague. It's unbelievably awful!"

The Public Relations office was down the fourth floor corridor from Chambrun's sanctum. Alison Barnwell was relatively new at the job. She had got the job under something of a handicap. She had been recommended for it by the Beaumont's owner, Mr. George Battle, that mysterious man of wealth who lived abroad and had not been inside this particular property of his for some fifteen years. Rumor had it that Mr. Battle was one of the four or five richest men in the world. The Beaumont was a multimillion dollar toy in his empire. There were odd rumors about Mr. Battle; that he never came to America because he was afraid to fly and was afraid to travel by boat for fear it would sink.

To be recommended for a job by Mr. Battle would not seem like a handicap on the face of things. A recommendation from him was like an order. And there was the rub. Pierre Chambrun ran the Beaumont and his staff was hand picked. To be pushed in over his head was not the best way to make friends and influence people at the Beaumont.

Alison's contact with Mr. George Battle was remote. A friend of her father's was a friend of Mr. Battle's. The friend had introduced Alison to Mr. Battle at a party in Cannes, where Alison was handling public relations for a moving picture company on location. The friend had suggested Alison for the job that was open at the Beaumont, flattering Mr. Battle that he

29

could judge people at a single glance. Mr. Battle, choosing to be a big shot at that moment, had looked at Alison and said "yes," which demonstrated something about his judgment. He had none. but he trusted the friend. In this instance the friend had made a good choice in suggesting Alison for the job. She didn't know the Beaumont, but she knew the kind of people who patronized it—the very, very rich—from other jobs. She had taste, a charming manner and the ability to assess what was the difference between good publicity and notoriety.

Chambrun had been cool and uncooperative in the beginning. Alison, with a dogged cheerfulness, refused to be brushed off. She came, in her ignorance of routines and protocol at the Beaumont, to Chambrun for advice and help. It wasn't long before the shrewd Chambrun recognized her real worth. He promptly thawed. He was only concerned with efficiency, and Alison had proved herself. There had even come a time between them of personal confidence. Chambrun was the only person in the Beaumont who knew that the smart and lovely Miss Barnwell was a widow, using her maiden name. Alison had been deeply in love with a young husband who had been killed under highly secret circumstances during some atomic experiments in the Nevada desert. Chambrun was aware that her brisk manner, the high, proud way she carried her lovely head, were all part of a gallant masquerade. The deep wounds of tragedy were not healed. He was also aware that this background contributed to Alison's effectiveness in her job. Staying busy round the clock kept her from too much introspective sorrow

It was shortly after her phone call from Sandy that Alison dropped by Chambrun's office.

"What a pleasant interruption," Chambrun said. "My battery needs recharging this morning, Alison."

His keen eyes took in the perfectly tailored skirt and

30

blouse. She managed to look expensive without having the money to be expensive. He'd always told himself that women had the responsibility to be attractive, and Alison met that responsibility in full sail.

"Sit down, my dear. Coffee?"

Alison wrinkled her nose. She was the only person in the hotel who had the courage to indicate that Chambrun's Turkish coffee was something less than nectar to her. "I need advice," she said. "I've seen nothing but green faces around the hotel this morning, and, come to think of it, you look a little green yourself. Having been summoned into the Presence for two o'clock this afternoon I need ammunition."

"Moon has sent for you?" Chambrun asked, pouring himself some coffee at the sideboard.

"Sent for, with warnings that the Great Man is in a lecherous mood."

"Don't go if you don't want to," Chambrun said. "I'll take over for you, if you like."

"Don't be silly," Alison said. "But I need to know just what's in the wind. I've only met Mr. Moon once in the Trapeze Bar. But I've seen him looking at me a good many times. It's unpleasantly like being undressed in public. What is he really like?"

Chambrun sat down behind his desk, and glanced over the rim of his coffee cup at Alison. Making love to her would have been a lovely experience some years ago. "I think it wouldn't be inaccurate to say that Moon is the most cordially disliked resident of this hotel in its history. And believe me, Alison, we've had some of the world's worst stinkers."

"Overdemanding?" she asked.

"The man is a sadist," Chambrun said. "No one is too small or unimportant to escape his notice: chambermaids, housekeepers, bellboys, elevator operators, telephone girls, clerks, waiters, captains—the whole

31

crew. To have to deal with him on the most insignificant issue is to take punishment."

"Is it against the rules to talk back?" Alison asked.

"Where it concerns the hotel, yes. If he gets personal, my dear, talk back all you like." Chambrun chuckled. "Someone did talk back in a way not too long ago. It's been Moon's practice to give a dinner party in the Grill about once a week. He's not generous with tips. He's abusive and contentious. One night he was taken ill at one of these parties and had to leave his guests. Two weeks later it happened again. I sent for the captain handling Moon's parties. 'No more Mickey Finns,' I told him."

Alison's blue eyes were dancing. "You mean they actually slipped him a Mickey?"

"I can't prove it," Chambrun said. "But he's stayed in excellent health since I warned my captain."

"He sounds like a crotchety old woman! What a delightful story!"

Chambrun lit a cigarette, his eyes heavy-lidded. "Never underestimate him, Alison. He's a very complex kind of heel—a dangerous heel. This party on Saturday night is for two hundred and fifty guests. I doubt very much if he cares anything for a single one of them. Thirty thousand dollars to entertain two hundred and fifty people you don't care about for probably less than four hours. Complex."

"Thirty thousand dollars!" Alison said, her eyes wide.

Chambrun shrugged. "Thirty thousand is conservative. Orchids flown in from Hawaii, special foods flown from Australia, Canada, Europe. The Metropolitan Opera Ensemble to sing 'Happy Birthday.' Individual gifts of gold compacts and gold lighters from Tiffany's. Two orchestras. Food, drinks, wines, gratuities. Yes, thirty thousand is too conservative. And for him it's not tax deductible. We handle four or five parties a year as big as this, but they're for big businesses that can write them off as promotion costs."

"But what does he get out of it?" Alison asked. "If he doesn't care for the people—?"

"I have to keep reminding you, my dear, that this is a luxury business. We deal in excesses from morning till night. Take Moon's apartment. He paid a hundred and ninety-four thousand dollars for it. Eight rooms, four baths, terrace on the roof. His annual maintenance charge is thirty-two thousand. Think of the kind of estate you could buy in the country for that kind of money." Chambrun reached in his desk drawer and brought out an elaborately printed folder. "We're expensive, Alison, but we aren't alone in this kind of thing. This is a brochure on the cooperative apartments at the Hotel Pierre. Just thumb through it. Here, you see? Eight rooms, five baths, one hundred and two thousand. Maintenance, twenty-three thousand. Here's another. One hundred and thirty thousand for eight rooms, five baths—with twenty-eight thousand in annual maintenance." Chambrun dropped the folder back in his drawer. "People spend this kind of money, Alison, to create a certain kind of image of themselves. Moon gives a thirty thousand dollar party because it perpetuates his image of himself. I admit you don't run into this kind of person on every street corner, but the woods are full of them, here and abroad. We happen to deal with a concentration of them here at the Beaumont."

"Wow!" Alison said.

Chambrun chuckled. "You know that display window in the lobby for the furriers? Before your time they had a little mechanical bear in the window. It sat at a table with a drink in front of it. The bear's nose would tilt down into the glass, rise up and tilt down again. You've seen that kind of gadget. When the nose is wet it tilts up, when it's dry it drops forward. Well, a South

33

American lady who was staying with us dropped in here to ask me how much the bear was. I hadn't the foggiest notion so I called the shop. One hundred and eighty-four dollars and forty-five cents, I was told. I told the lady, with my best expression of regret. An outrageous price for a toy. 'Please have twelve sent to my home in Ecuador,' she said to me, blandly. 'I want them for my grandchildren.' And out she walked, her image of a kindly grandmother intact. Never be surprised in this business, Alison, by the mention of sums of money. Just when you think you've heard the end in extravagance, somebody will come up with a topper."

Alison shook her head. "At least you've helped to put Mr. Moon in perspective," she said. "What kind of suggestions should I be prepared to make to him?"

"He'll tell you exactly what he wants," Chambrun said. "Aubrey Moon always knows exactly what he wants—and gets it." His eyes narrowed. "Knowing you, my dear. I suspect you may come up with a First. I doubt if you'll find him attractive."

Alison stood up. Her laughter was warm and infectious. "Did I ever tell you I studied jujitsu in college? We were led to believe we'd have to use it often." Her eyes clouded. "I became a one-man woman too soon to find out if they were right."

She walked into the outer office and literally bounced off a young man who was standing by Chambrun's secretary's desk.

"I am sorry," she said. "Daydreaming!"

Alison was tall for a girl, and this young man was about eye-level with her. His eyes were gray, she noticed, with a little network of wrinkles at their corners. It was hard to tell whether he was young-old, or old-young. His hair was fair, and crew-cut. His mouth was unpleasantly hard until he smiled, and then his whole expression became warm with good humor.

"It was a kind of pleasure," he said.

British-sounding, Alison thought, as she walked down the corridor to her office.

FOUR

Pierre Chambrun's boss, the absent Mr. George Battle, might not be the best instant judge of character, but after twenty years of managing the Beaumont, Chambrun himself could add up a stranger about as quickly and accurately as anyone you could name. He had seen all types and all kinds come and go over the years and he could classify them, insofar as the hotel was concerned, almost without error. Were they likely to be dead beats? Were they living beyond their normal means in staying at the Beaumont? Were they likely to be troublesome lushes? Complainers? Was it possible they were in some racket for which they needed the Beaumont as a backdrop? And, vaguely, did they feel "right" or "wrong"?

The young man with the blond crew-cut, the crow's-footed eyes which suggested much outdoors and sun, and the hard mouth with unexpected laughter lines at its corners, drew only one negative mark on Chambrun's preliminary score card. The Beaumont's prices—forty dollars a day for a single room—would be a little rich for his blood in the normal course of events. Possibly not for a brief holiday.

Chambrun glanced down at the letter the young man had brought him.

Dear Pierre:

   Any courtesies you can show to my young friend, John Wills, will be deeply appreciated.

Best regards,
Tony Vail

35

Anthony Vail had once been Chambrun's assistant at the Beaumont and was now resident manager of the Chadwick House in London. Chambrun made up his mind. He lifted his heavy eyelids and smiled at John Wills.

"How is Tony?" he asked.

"First class when I saw him last, sir." Wills' voice was soft and pleasant. Somehow, while his speech sounded British, it wasn't quite right.

"You're an Englishman, Mr. Wills?"

"No, sir. American. Born in Columbus, Ohio. But I've spent big hunks of my life in England. My father represented one of the big rubber companies over there. London manager. He joined the British Army at the outbreak of the last war. My mother and I were sent home. After the war we went back."

"Your father came through all right, then?"

"He came through the war." A little nerve twitched high up on Wills' cheek. "He died in 1950. My mother stayed on in England until she died some months ago. I've been back and forth."

"Well, what can I do for you, Mr. Wills?"

Wills took a cigarette out of his pocket and lit it. Chambrun felt himself being studied. Anyone who could read anything behind his hooded eyes was welcome.

"I've done a bit of everything, Mr. Chambrun," he said. "I was too young for the big war myself. Did my stretch over here. Eighteen months in Korea. Flyer. Difficult to find a career after that. Education interrupted. It's a common story today."

"All too common," Chambrun said.

"I'm thirty-three now," Wills said, as though that was very old.

"Lucky you," Chambrun said.

"Quite by accident I've come into a pretty good thing. Some chaps I know are going into the luxury business. Round-the-world stuff. I'd be the director of one of these tours each six months. But I need to know my stuff."

Chambrun's fingers did a little dance on the edge of his desk. Something of Wills' first directness was missing. He didn't meet Chambrun's eyes as he told his story. Something off-beat here, Chambrun told himself. Maybe it was just embarrassment at not being settled at what he considered was maturity. Maybe.

Wills smiled suddenly, and it was completely disarming. "I've never spent much time in luxury hotels and resorts, sir. Not my dish—and we never had the money for it. Now I need to know what makes them tick. Tony said this was the luxury hotel in the world. What I want, sir, if it isn't asking too much, is the privilege of just floating around, seeing how things work, the inside machinery, the—the philosophy of the business, if you see what I mean."

"That shouldn't be much of a problem," Chambrun said. "How much time do you want to put into it?"

"Just a week, sir. Through Saturday."

"Where are you staying?"

"I've already checked in here, sir."

"Well, first of all, I'll put you in the hands of my Public Relations director. She knows the hotel from top to bottom, can introduce you to the various department heads, everyone you might want to talk to. That will have to wait, however, until tomorrow morning. She's tied up this afternoon with something, which, by the way, might be an interesting take-off point for you. You've heard of Aubrey Moon, of course?"

Wills' blue eyes were suddenly bright and diamond-hard. "Yes, I know who he is, of course."

"He's giving a birthday party for two hundred and fifty guests in our ballroom on Saturday night. The party will cost him from thirty to forty thousand dollars. It's a luxury operation in spades, Mr. Wills. Perhaps if

37

I had Miss Barnwell set you up to follow the preparation and carrying through of that operation, you'd see the whole business running in high gear."

"I'd like that very much," Wills said. "The party angle would be very much up my street."

"Fine. I'll set up an appointment with Miss Barnwell in the morning. Meanwhile, get yourself oriented. I'll give my house officer a ring. Fellow named Jerry Dodd. Ex-cop. Anything you want to see, any place you want to go, Jerry'll fix it for you. Then, tomorrow—Miss Barnwell."

"I don't know how to thank you, Mr. Chambrun."

"It's nothing. Tell you the truth I'm proud to show off the place to someone who's interested in its mechanics."

John Wills walked down the hallway to the bank of elevators. His mouth felt dry. It was difficult to lie so blandly to a decent guy like Chambrun. He wondered how Chambrun would react if he knew that he had just finished helping to make the arrangements for a possible murder in his hotel.

It was exactly three minutes to two when Alison Barnwell rang the doorbell of Penthouse M. Perversely, perhaps, she had worn her most attractive afternoon dress which showed off her elegant figure to perfection. One good thing her job made possible was the buying of clothes at a discount, and she had entrée to a designer who would sell his models after they'd been shown at throwaway prices. If Aubrey Moon was in a lecherous mood Alison decided she would make his disappointment as acute as she could. The old goat! Seventy-five on Saturday!

Sandy Stewart opened the door. At the sight of Alison she sucked in her breath. "You should have sent someone else. Alison," she said, in a stage whisper.

"Don't be absurd, darling. This is my job."

"He's sending me out."

"Have fun," Alison said. "Any time I can't outrun a seventy-five year old gent I'd better retire to a nunnery."

"You don't know him," Sandy said.

"I know me," Alison said, crisply. "Let's not keep the Great Man waiting."

Alison wasn't quite sure what she'd expected, but the sight of Aubrey Moon, wrapped in a Japanese robe, reclining on his throne, a pot of incense smoking on the table beside him, sipping his iced coconut milk and holding a cigarette in a long, jade holder, produced an almost irresistible impulse to laugh. The beady black eyes in their heavy pouches acted as a check. Quite unexpectedly Alison felt a little shiver run along her spine. There was a kind of naked evil here, she thought.

"I'm glad to see that you regard time as an unexpendable commodity, Miss Barnwell," Moon said. His voice was thin and faraway, and yet, at the same time, strong and tense as piano wire.

"My time as well as yours, Mr. Moon," Alison said, sweetly.

"That will be all, Sandy," Moon said, without looking at his secretary. "Two hours on your own."

"If there's anything—" Sandy began.

"There's nothing!" Moon said, giving her an irritable gesture of dismissal with a slender white hand. "Do sit down, Miss Barnwell."

"Thank you." Alison sat. She took a small notebook and a gold pencil from her alligator-skin bag. She looked up, expectantly bright, at the Great Man.

Moon studied her in a leisurely way. He was evidently pleased with what he saw. "I hope you're not here loaded with hostility for me, Miss Barnwell."

"Hostility? Why should I feel hostility, Mr. Moon? We've scarcely exchanged six words up to now."

"Oh come, Miss Barnwell. Strangers are conditioned

to hate me—by my friends and enemies. I could see in Sandy's face that she'd warned you that I'd allowed myself some comments on your attractiveness, even wondered aloud how friendly you might be. This would send poor puritanical Sandy into a swivet. And I can hear the good Chambrun warning you that I am decadent and vicious. But saints are, as a rule, rather dull, don't you think?"

"I've never known any," Alison said.

"My character assassins are, usually, hypocrites," Moon said. He seemed to be trying to come to some conclusion about her. "My philosophy of life is, perhaps, a little shocking to the prudes and conformists, Miss Barnwell. I have been called a sadist for telling the truth about the weak and uncertain people who run our world. But you see, most of us are brought up on the myth that God is Love. God countenances wars, He countenances cruelties, He countenances the exploitation of the weak, He countenances the destruction of the helpless by sending droughts, and hurricanes, and floods, and blights to our growing things. For thousands of years man has lied and, at the same time, raised his hand and said: 'May God strike me dead if I'm not telling the truth.' And nowhere in history is there a recorded instance of God striking anyone dead for telling a lie. Hate is the key to God, and hate is the key to man. Most men cover their basic hatreds and hostilities with a sham nobility. The truth about Aubrey Moon? He has never pretended to nobility, nor attempted to hide the hatred and hostility which is at the core of his nature. So Aubrey Moon probably comes closer to being an honest man than any other human being of your acquaintance, Miss Barnwell."

Alison looked straight at him. "So people hate you for not pretending to a nobility you haven't got?"   .

"As they pretend, Miss Barnwell. As they pretend."

"And so to punish them, you play God—your kind

40

of God—and send droughts and hurricanes and floods and blights to destroy them."

The black eyes glittered. "Do I detect a faint note of impertinence, Miss Barnwell?"

She smiled at him. "I'm the impertinence type, Mr. Moon, except at my job—which is publicity. Shall we get to it?"

"You are something of a surprise, Miss Barnwell," Moon said. "There is more to you to reckon with than a pretty face and well formed breasts. I shall have to give it my consideration. In the meanwhile, as you suggest, let's get down to how we shall publicly handle my celebration."

Alison sat very still, pencil poised over her notebook, praying that no color had risen to her cheeks to betray the sudden fierce outrage she felt.

About twenty minutes before Alison's interview with Aubrey Moon began, one of the operators in the telephone switchboard office on the third floor got a red signal from room 609.

"Yes, please?"

A woman's voice, sounding small and detached, asked: "Would you send up a telephone book to 609, please."

"What telephone book, Miss? You have the four New York City books in the rack under the table beside your bed."

"Oh." A pause. "Well, could you send me the Boston book?"

"May I look up the number for you, Miss?"

"Please—I want the book."

"At once, Miss." And as she flipped her connecting cords loose: "Who's in 609?"

Mrs. Veach, at the chief operator's desk, checked a card file. "A Miss Pamela Prym. New to us, so far as I know."

"She wants a Boston phone book sent up."

The book was dispatched by a bellman. Twenty minutes of normal switchboard action went by and then the red light from 609 flashed on the board. The small voice was there.

"I wonder if you could send me the—the Chicago telephone book?"

This time the operator didn't bother with questions. "At once, Miss." No matter how irritating or unusual the service asked at the Beaumont it was given.

"Maybe she's practicing her reading," the bellman remarked drily as he took up the second phone book within a half an hour.

Twenty minutes after that the red signal from 609 showed up on the board again.

"Could you—could you send me the Philadelphia telephone directory, please?"

"Of course, Miss." The connection cords flipped loose. "Crazy witch," the operator muttered as she sent for the bellman to make his third trip.

Mrs. Veach had been handling odd requests over the switchboard for a good many years. Somewhere, in some subconscious corner of her orderly mind, were danger signals. Danger to the hotel, which was her life. It was perhaps fifteen minutes after the third phone book had gone up that Mrs. Veach got up abruptly from her desk and walked over behind the operator who handled the sixth floor.

"Any out calls from 609, Flo?"

"No, Mrs. Veach. She's just collecting phone books, I guess."

"Connect me with Mr. Chambrun," Mrs. Veach said sharply, and went back to her desk.

Chambrun's cheerful came over the wire a moment later. "Yes, Mrs. Veach?"

"609 has sent down for three out-of-town phone books," Mrs. Veach reported. "A Miss Pamela Prym, according to the registration card. There have been no outgoing calls, sir. I wondered—"

"An avid letter writer in search of addresses?" Chambrun suggested.

"Another thought occurred to me, sir," Mrs. Veach said, outwardly placid. "They could be used to stand on."

Chambrun's voice went hard. "Thank you, Mrs. Veach. Have Jerry Dodd meet me on the sixth floor with a pass key."

There was no response to a sharp knocking on the door of 609 when Chambrun and the house officer met there. Jerry Dodd used the pass key and let them in.

"Save us!" Jerry said, under his breath.

Miss Pamela Prym's naked heels dangled some distance from the floor. A chair, on which had been stacked seven telephone books, had been kicked over. Miss Prym had hung herself with the belt from a terry-cloth robe.

Suicides in a big hotel are not unheard of. Jerry Dodd cut Miss Prym down and laid her on the bed. It was instantly apparent that artificial respiration was useless. They went through the routine of calling the police and sending for the oxygen tank and mask kept in the infirmary on the second floor. It was routine, because Miss Prym was very, very dead.

"Never knew her name before," Jerry Dodd said, when he had finally given up all efforts to revive the girl.

"You know who she is?" Chambrun asked.

"Call girl," Jerry said. "Hundred and fifty buck a night gal. Most everybody in the place knows her by sight. We just call her The Duchess."

Chambrun's first thought was that he would have to fire the night registration clerk. You didn't rent rooms in the Beaumont to known professionals. Then he remembered that Karl Nevers, the regular night man, had been off, sick. One of the day men had substituted. He would have had no reason to refuse a Miss Pamela Prym.

The only luggage Miss Prym had brought was a small overnight bag. Her purse lay open on the bureau. Chambrun glanced through it for some sort of formal identification. Beyond a lipstick, compact and some keys the purse contained only a registered letter, addressed to Miss Pamela Prym at an address a few blocks from the Beaumont. The name and address were typewritten on an ordinary post office stamped envelope. The return address was a post office box at the General Post Office.

The letter itself was typewritten on a piece of white typewriter bond of a reasonably good grade. As Chambrun read it his lips pursed in a soundless whistle.

December 20.

Dear Miss Prym:

I am well aware of your hatred for Aubrey Moon. I also know the exact state of your finances. I have a proposition that may satisfy your thirst for revenge and your need for money.

At this moment there is deposited to your account at the Waltham Trust Company on Madison Avenue the sum of $10,000. (Ten thousand.) You may draw it today. You may use it in any way you choose. You may pay your debts with it, or skip the country, or light bonfires with it. You will have earned the right to the money if Aubrey Moon is dead two months from today, February 20th to be precise. If you take the money and he is not dead by midnight on February 20th you will not live through the following day yourself.

If you do not take the money you will live— but you will regret many, many times having

44

missed the chance to be free of Moon, free of poverty, free of degradation.

There was no signature, typewritten or otherwise. Chambrun passed the note over to Jerry Dodd without comment.

"Some kind of a practical joke," Jerry said. "If you want to pay ten G's to get someone killed you don't hire a neurotic call girl. You can find yourself a good professional killer for half that dough."

"You know if Moon was one of her customers?" Chambrun asked.

"About twice a month, according to the night crew, she spent an hour or two with him."

"I should get around more," Chambrun said, drily. "This is the fifteenth. She had six days left, counting today, but she threw in the towel. I suppose she knew she couldn't go through with it and chose this grim way to fight back."

"For ten G's I'd of taken a crack at the Great Man myself!" Jerry said.

By six-thirty that night the news of the suicide at The Beaumont was public property. The death of an obscure call girl in a big hotel wouldn't ordinarily get space outside the tabloids. But the extraordinary note found in her bag, connecting her with Aubrey Moon, a world celebrity, made it a big story. "PLOT TO KILL FAMOUS WRITER."

A version of it came over the six-thirty news on television. In a single room on the fourteenth floor of the Beaumont, John Wills was stretched out on his bed, hands locked behind his head, watching the news broadcast on his TV set.

Suddenly he sat bolt upright on the bed as the announcer began reading the note Miss Prym had left behind her. He went over and switched off the set. There

45

were little beads of perspiration on his forehead. He turned on the light over his bureau and opened a middle drawer. It was filled with clean shirts.

He lifted several shirts until he came on a blue silk scarf, neatly folded, which had been placed between a layer of shirts. He took the scarf out and unfolded it on top of his bureau. In the scarf was a passport folder and a small, compact automatic.

He opened the folder, and from one of its pockets he took a sheet of white paper. He began to read it, his lips moving.

December 20.

My dear John Wills:

I am well aware of your hatred for Aubrey Moon. I also know the exact state of your finances. I have a proposition that may satisfy your thirst for revenge and your need for money.

At this moment there is deposited to your account at the Waltham Trust Company on Madison Avenue the sum of $10,000. (Ten thousand.) You may draw it today. You may use it in any way you choose—

Wills' eyes skipped down to the bottom of the page.

If you take the money and he is not dead by midnight February 20th you will not live through the following day yourself—

With stiff fingers Wills refolded the paper and put it back with his passport. For a moment his right hand rested on the automatic, feeling the fit of it in his palm.

"What kind of nonsense is this?" he said out loud.

46

PART 2

THE POLICE LIEUTENANT, whose name was Hardy, was not impressed by Aubrey Moon's fame. Hardy was a big, dark, athletic-looking young man who looked more like a good-natured, if slightly puzzled, college fullback than a Homicide detective. The Oriental treasures in Moon's living room, the faint aroma of incense, the man himself, reclining on his throne, all added up to fakery in young Mr. Hardy's mind. Some kind of queer, he probably told himself.

Aubrey Moon reacted to the police lieutenant as he might have to an irritating fly. The Great Man had withdrawn behind the puffy mask of his face, his emotions—if any—unreadable.

"We've made inquiries at the Waltham Trust Company, Mr. Moon," Hardy said. "Ten thousand dollars was deposited there, presumably by Miss Pamela Prym, and subsequently withdrawn by her."

"You say 'presumably' deposited by her, Lieutenant? Can't you do better than that? Who did deposit it—when, how. 'Presumably,' my foot!"

"We're checking it out," Hardy said.

"Bully for you," Moon said in a bored voice.

"Who could hate you enough to pay ten thousand dollars to have you killed?" Hardy asked.

Moon's smile was distant. "Hundreds of people,

Lieutenant. Oh, literally hundreds."

"This is no laughing matter," Hardy said.

"That depends on where you sit, Lieutenant. To me the picture of poor Pamela slipping a knife between my ribs as she lay beside me on my couch, or poisoning my drink, or perhaps garroting me with a bit of picture wire is highly comical. She had a talented body, but the mind of a small, sentimental child of eight."

A sharp hissing sound came from the corner of the room. It was Pierre Chambrun letting his breath out between his teeth. He had come with Hardy to the penthouse. He seemed uncharacteristically disturbed by the tragedy of Miss Pamela Prym.

"Ten thousand bucks isn't hay," Hardy said. "Surely there aren't hundreds of people who hate you that much, Mr. Moon."

"I should be very much disappointed if there weren't," Moon said.

"For God's sake let's cut the comedy," Hardy said.

Moon turned his head to look with weary contempt at the lieutenant. "My dear young man, someone is willing to pay handsomely to see to it that I am dead before I enter upon my seventy-sixth year. He is an idiot if he put all his eggs in one basket—if I may refer to Pamela as a basket. She was a most unlikely choice. I suggest you find out who else may have sudden new bank accounts."

"You're suggesting someone else may have been offered money for the job?" Hardy asked, frowning.

Moon chuckled. "If I wanted to be certain of the death of someone comparable to Aubrey Moon—making the unlikely assumption that there is someone comparable to Aubrey Moon—I would have more than one string to my bow—and damn the expense! It must be obvious to you, Lieutenant, that I need protection. Your superiors will not, I think, be happy if you assume the danger is past with the suicide of poor little Pamela."

"If you feel you're in danger," Chambrun said, in a flat, colorless voice, "perhaps you'd be well advised to cancel your party. You'll be a prime target in the center of two hundred and fifty uncheckable guests."

"My dear Chambrun, nobody is going to tell me what to do or force me to alter my plans. It is up to you, as resident manager of the hotel, and the lieutenant here, to see to my safety."

"Party? What party?" Hardy asked.

"Mr. Moon is planning to celebrate the miracle of his survival for seventy-five years," Chambrun said. "In the Grand Ball Room with two hundred and fifty guests. Saturday night."

"I don't think the Commissioner will allow you to run that kind of risk if this isn't cleared up," Hardy said.

"Allow me?" Moon's eyes had a bright glitter in them. "It would be interesting to see him try to stop me. I choose to celebrate, and I will celebrate—here at the Beaumont, or elsewhere if Mr. Chambrun wishes to explain to his board of directors why he proposes to give up a very substantial piece of business."

Chambrun shrugged. "It's your life, Mr. Moon. If you choose to risk it, I, personally, couldn't care less."

Moon chuckled, softly. "You see how it is, Lieutenant? Nobody loves me."

"I don't see how it is," Hardy said, stubbornly. "You're not taking this seriously. What do you know about it that you haven't told us?"

"I don't know anything about it," Moon said, "except that someone is playing a rather expensive joke on me. I am supposed to run for cover, hiding my head under my wing—making a public spectacle of myself. Well, to quote a great statesman who will never be quoted for anything else he said: 'I do not choose to run.' "

There was no question about how Pamela Prym, the unfortunate call girl with the unlikely name, had died. It was a suicide. Lieutenant Hardy was only concerned with the threat to Moon, contained in the note found in Miss Prym's bag. Instinct told him it was a joke—a monstrous joke that had unintentionally led to a suicide. But the joke theory stuck in Hardy's craw when he thought of the money. Ten thousand dollars had been deposited to Miss Prym's account at the Waltham Trust and she had drawn it and used it. In Hardy's frame of reference there was nothing funny about ten thousand dollars.

They were back in Chambrun's office from where Hardy had made a telephone report to the Police Commissioner. Moon's involvement in the case was blowing a cold wind down official corridors.

Hardy glanced at the girl Chambrun had summoned. Miss Alison Barnwell was quite a dish, the lieutenant thought. But he wondered if she was tough enough to act as press representative for the hotel in a situation like this.

"It's not our job to protect him," Chambrun was saying to Alison, his voice hard. "Our job is to protect the hotel. Damage has already been done. The suicide story will be in the evening papers and is already on everyone's radio and TV set. The tie-in with Moon makes it front page. Every reporter and gossip columnist in town will be camped on our doorsteps for the next few days." He pointed irritably to a memo on his desk. "Willard Storm is already yelling for an interview with me."

Willard Storm was the bright new young man about town. His daily column, which he called "Storm Center," was pushing Winchell, Sullivan and the other old-timers. Storm stood for a kind of journalism Chambrun hated. Story at any cost, no matters who it hurts.

"There's a kind of lunacy involved here," Hardy said. "I guess you have to think like a nut to match wits with one."

Alison's finely boned face was pale. "Like the lieutenant, it's hard for me to think of this as a joke," she said. "Ten thousand dollars!"

Chambrun made an impatient gesture. "Sums of money shouldn't surprise you in this job. Alison. I gave you a little lecture on that subject this morning. The hotel is loaded with people to whom ten thousand dollars is pocket money. It may look like a year's salary to you; to them it's something to take on a shopping tour." He brought his fist down on the desk. "You know something about this job?" His voice was angry. "It makes you the damnedest rooter for people without limitless bank accounts. You see some of the stenographers or sales girls from the shops looking in the display windows in the lobby. You know they're dreaming of a day that won't come when they could buy something they see. And while they're standing there some fat, rich bitch elbows past them and buys six of whatever it is. Take our telephone operators. They have the lives of hundreds of cheating males and females in the palms of their hands. They keep the wrong calls from going through at the wrong time. They take clandestine messages. They're tucked away in an office on the third floor. Do you know they're lucky if they get five dollars a year in tips? The rich expect to be served. Let one wrong call get through, let one secret message be indiscreetly delivered, and they'll be clamoring at me for the girl's blood. Take Amato, our banquet manager. He's got ulcers. They'll be bleeding before the week's out because Moon will choose to make a whipping boy out of him. Moon's dinner will be perfection, but Amato will take a beating all the same. I hate the super-rich! I hate whoever it is who can afford to dish out ten thousand dollar tips to drive a girl like Prym to hang herself. She could be driven to despair because she's a paid cog in a pleasure machine that must work for them night and day, year in and year out."

"And we," Alison said, her eyes suddenly dancing, "are the chief engineers of that pleasure machine. The Hotel Beaumont, Playground Of The Rich In New York. It says so right in our brochure."

"All right!" Chambrun said, still angry. "So we're pimps for the rich. But we don't have to kiss their feet!"

In his room on the fourteenth floor John Wills was stretched out on his bed once more, staring up through cigarette smoke at the ceiling. The crow's-feet at the corners of his gray eyes were contracted as if he were in pain. It was pain, and he had lived with it for twelve years, raw and never healing.

"John Wills" was his legal name, made so by the courts, but he had been born John MacIver. The name MacIver would have rung a bell with Chambrun. It would have rung a bell with any newspaperman who had been working at his job in 1950. The name of Captain Warren MacIver, cashiered out of the British Army for having an adulterous relationship with the wife of his commanding officer, had got star billing from all press services. It was not an ordinary adultery. The court-martial attempted to prove that Warren MacIver had not been interested in a love affair, but had been using the Colonel's lady to get at top secret information in the Colonel's possession. Since the Colonel was involved with "the Bomb," Warren MacIver was classified as a top-drawer villain, despite his plea of innocence. MacIver denied, as he naturally would, having an affair with the lady, and violently denied the charge of espionage. His case was damaged by a rather absurd outburst from the witness box by the lady in the case, who declared that the man with whom she'd been having an affair was the famous author, journalist and world traveler, Aubrey Moon. It was absurd because the manager of a certain hotel, a housemaid and a room-service waiter all testified that Warren MacIver was the man who had signed the register with a false "Mr. and Mrs." and had been seen in compromising positions with the lady in the hotel suite. Moon wasn't even called as a witness. He was as familiar to the British public as a film star. No one could confuse his dark, saturnine elegance with the blond Captain MacIver.

The charge of espionage wasn't proved, though the public had little doubt it was fact. Sage remarks about "smoke and fire" were passed around freely. MacIver was dishonorably discharged from the service. Two years later Captain Warren MacIver shot himself in a small hotel room in Liverpool.

Captain MacIver had been John Wills' father. Wills had been his mother's maiden name.

John Wills had been with the United States Army in Korea at the time of his father's disaster. The factual news he got was sketchy. The sensational aspect of the case seemed to come in floods. Wills' personal relationships were affected. His brother flyers didn't want to talk about it, which resulted in a kind of isolation. Actually he felt that he was distrusted. He was the son of a spy, even though the spy charges were eventually not proved.

Letters from his mother were censored, but the heartbreak for her came through. One thing she made clear. She believed in her husband, she loved him, she would stand by him no matter what.

John Wills' relationship with his father had been twisted out of normal by the war. Warren MacIver had joined the British Army in '39. His family had gone back to America for the duration. John was ten. For seven years his only contact with his father was by letter. When America entered the war in '41 MacIver, through some wire pulling, stayed in the British service. He was an expert with bombs. For all the years of the terrible blitzing of London, Warren MacIver had been engaged in the suicidal business of deactivating unexploded bombs that fell on the city. It required a kind of steel nerve, a kind of heroism that only people close to disaster could understand. Little John saw him as the most gallant of heroes in his imagination. When Warren MacIver was decorated by the King himself he grew into a Bunyanesque figure in John's mind.

The MacIvers were reunited in England in '47. John was eighteen that summer. Warren MacIver had stayed on in the British Army because jobs were hard to come by and because his special knowledge made him valuable in the incredible preparations already being made for the next war.

Warren MacIver was not what his son had expected. He was a quiet, introspective man, with none of the dash or glamor young John had anticipated. But what he lacked in public glamor he made up for in a deep warmth, a shy friendliness, a complete understanding of John's difficulty to adjust to a father after eight years. They walked London together. They made expeditions into the country for some fishing. They grew close without ever putting it into words. And there was another thing of which Wills reminded himself over and over in the black days in Korea when the news about his father was filtering in. He thought he had never seen two people so deeply in love, so perfectly in tune, as his father and mother. That Warren MacIver could have been carrying on an affair, for whatever reason, with another woman was hard to believe. But war did strange things to men. In his own group he knew fellows who carried around pictures of their wives, some of them with small children, who were driven to find romantic outlets they wouldn't have thought of in peacetime.

The MacIver case was embalmed in newspaper files when John finished his term of service, was discharged and finally got back to England. He was shocked by what he found. His parents were living in a cheap little flat in the Streatham section of London. Since being cashiered from the army Warren MacIver hadn't been able to hold a job. Each time he got something he was fired before he could really get his teeth into it.

"It's almost as if someone followed him around, waiting for him to find something, and then sprung a trap under him," John's mother told him.

MacIver was a beaten man. He looked physically ill. John would catch his father's eyes on him, only to have them move quickly away. John seemed unable to assure him that he believed in him. The trouble was there was nothing to believe in. His father wouldn't discuss the case. Once, in almost tearful anger, he said: "You have to take me at face value, Johnny. I've denied it all so many times. There's no point in denying it to you again."

But there came a time when Warren MacIver made a decision which was unknown to his wife and son. He couldn't go on. There was the possibility of a job in Liverpool, he told them. Why he had chosen Liverpool as a place to die, John never knew. His father suggested they take one of their old-time walks through the city on the day before he was due to go to Liverpool to "investigate the job."

They walked for miles without talking. Occasionally MacIver would point to some building or vacant lot as a place where he'd worked on a live and ticking bomb in the old days. They finally wound up in a little pub on the outskirts of the city somewhere, tired, hungry and thirsty. It was there, over a beer and some cold meat, cheese and bread, that Warren MacIver told the story to his son. It came about in the most casual way. John, struggling for something to talk about when all either of them had on their minds was the unmentionable tragedy, had commented on the fact that London still showed many scars of the blitzing.

"It's hard to understand how people who lived through it will permit it to happen again," he said. "They lived through it, yet they take for truth every word a politican or statesman says today and calmly allow themselves to be dragged back into war again."

"The truth is a funny thing," Warren MacIver said. "I used to think it had substance. I used to say 'The Nelson monument was built in such and such a year,' and know that was true. But the Russians rewrite history, and presently, for the Russian people, what we know today is a lie will become the truth. I wonder if our historians may not have done the same thing in the past? The truth, somehow, isn't absolute. The truth is what we believe today, whether it has any basis in historical fact or not." He was filling an old blackened pipe from a plastic pouch. "I ought to know!" he said, with a bitterness so intense John could feel the pain of it personally.

Somehow John had the sense not to speak. For the first time since he'd come home he felt his father was ready to talk. But when MacIver began to talk again it seemed for a moment he had been wrong.

"Back in '45," MacIver said. "I was at my job—scurrying about the city where unexploded bombs were reported; literally listening to them through a stethoscope; unscrewing a delicate fusecap, knowing that perhaps if you coughed you'd be blown into eternity. It was a nervy business, Johnny. When you had a little time off you relaxed. I relaxed by getting royally crocked.

"One night a bomb hit the Brunswick House Hotel. In the middle of a blitz you did what came to hand. I found myself part of an emergency crew holding a fireman's net outside the upper windows of the hotel for people to jump into. I remember seeing a man at a window on the third or fourth floor. He was fighting like a maniac with a woman and a couple of kids. He managed to push them out of the way and jump first. When we yanked him out of the net I recognized him. It was Aubrey Moon, the famous writer and war correspondent. I knew him from his picture in the papers and newsreels. Incidentally, the woman and her kids made it just before the whole wing collapsed. But no thanks to Moon."

For the first time in his life John heard stark hatred in his father's voice as he mentioned Moon's name.

"Week or so later I was off duty," MacIver said. "Moon turned up at our officer's mess as a guest. He was a big shot. People all over the world were crying into their breakfast tea over his accounts of the courage of the Londoner, stolidly going about his job in the midst of almost nightly death from the sky. It was good stuff, touching stuff. Our commanding officer asked Moon to make a little speech. He chose to tell the story of the bombing of the Brunswick House, of the heroism of the people, and, modestly, of his own heroism in saving a good many lives." MacIver drew a deep breath. "I was tight, Johnny. We didn't like phony heroes in those days. I got up on my feet and told what I'd seen. It was bad manners, but I didn't give a damn. It made me sick to hear him blow his own horn when I knew what a coward he was. It made him look very cheap, and I got a public reprimand for it— and an unofficial pat on the back from my C.O. Naturally I knew I hadn't made a friend. I didn't realize I'd made an enemy who had the power, the influence, and above all the money, to hold me down until I was dead—or he was dead."

MacIver held a match to his pipe with an unsteady hand. "Do you know something, Johnny? I've never laid eyes on Moon in the flesh from that day to this. But he's been on my back every single minute of time since then—seven mortal years."

John still kept silent, afraid he'd break the spell, dam up this first flow of words.

"You know why I stayed on in the army after the war," MacIver went on, after a moment. "No job. I'd developed special abilities the service could use. I was assigned to a new regiment. The commanding officer had been a temporary general in the war, reduced now to the permanent rank of colonel. He acted as though the whole world had been responsible for his demotion. He was a stuffy bastard. He'd been lucky enough to marry an extremely attractive young woman. She served under him in the woman's auxiliary—WATS. Maybe she was taken by his gold braid and all that posh that went with his wartime job. She was stuck with him. Your mother and I had to see them socially on occasions. I liked the girl. Her name was Kathleen. When I say liked her, Johnny, I liked her as you might someone who works in the same office with you, or that you meet every day commuting to your job. There was nothing between us. Absolutely nothing. That's a bit of history that's been rewritten, Johnny—so that a lie has become the truth.

"One night there was a dance at a big private house somewhere. I danced with Kathleen—duty dance. All the junior officers danced with their C.O.'s wife as a duty. I noticed she was tight that night, with a kind of wild desperate look to her. She asked me to take her out on the terrace for a breath of air. Why she chose me to blow up to I don't know. It was mixed up and wild. She couldn't stand the Colonel. She was in love with someone else. She had to get free somehow. She needed someone to talk to. Would I help her? Would I be her friend?

"Of course I said 'yes,' without thinking it meant anything important. The next day she called me. Would I come to the Russell Square Hotel, room 6B. It bothered me. I didn't want to get involved with some almost-stranger's marriage difficulties. But she sounded so desperately in need of help. I went."

MacIver's pipe had gone out. He started to reach for his lighter, changed his mind and put the pipe down on the table. John saw that his father's hands were shaking.

"I went to the hotel," MacIver said, slowly. "I went up to 6B and knocked on the door. Kathleen was there, drunk and hysterical. I had to slap her down before she made any sense. Then she told me. The man she was in love with was Moon. He must have been in his early sixties, but somehow celebrities like him seem to be ageless. I suppose he'd dazzled her with promises of a house in London, a villa in Cannes, a yacht, an apartment in New York, clothes, jewels—God knows what. She wasn't much of a girl, I guess, to be taken in by that sort of thing. Who knows? The point was Moon had walked out on her, left her flat. She was in a suicidal state of mind.

"Into the middle of this hassle walked the Colonel, the hotel manager, and a private detective. The Colonel jumped to the conclusion that I was the 'Mr. Wilson' registered there with 'Mrs. Wilson,' his wife. I denied it, of course. I must say for Kathleen, she denied it—then and later. She told the truth. That the man who'd kept this suite for the last month or two in the name of 'Wilson' was Aubrey Moon. Do you know what happened then, Johnny? A hotel clerk swore I'd been the one to sign the register. The maid and a room service waiter testified to having seen me in the room in various informal attitudes with Kathleen. They looked at Kathleen, pityingly. Everybody knew Aubrey Moon by sight. No one could possibly mistake him for me.

"I—I didn't know what hit me, Johnny. I was court-martialed on perjured testimony. Luckily the espionage charge didn't hold up. But that hasn't been enough for Moon. It's his intention to discredit me, drive me out of England. I haven't been able to hold a job. The minute I get one I'm fired. Moon might be in Tibet, but if I got something there was someone on his payroll on hand to see to it I got the sack. Endless, endless persecution for seven years, Johnny. I went to him once. He laughed at me; reminded me of that day in the officer's mess when I'd made a fool of him. I knew that day he'd never let up. I knew that day there was no way to fight his kind of money and influence. No one could be allowed to puncture his vanity and survive. I've learned one thing out of it, Johnny. There's no way to fight money. A man with money can have his way, whether his way is honorable or dishonorable. For a while I'd hoped he'd get tired of the trouble it must take to keep his foot on my neck. I know now he never will."

John spoke after a long silence. "There's one thing I don't understand, sir. It was pure luck he found you in the lady's room at the Russell Square."

Warren MacIver shook his head wearily. "He was ready to break with Kathleen. He was having her watched. Someone must have been listening that night when she asked if I would help. It must have delighted him to find he could kill two birds with one stone. He waited for her to call me and ask me to come to the hotel. His bought witnesses were waiting. The Colonel was notified, the trap sprung." MacIver looked up at his son. "That's the truth, Johnny; the whole, un-varnished truth. However you hear it told sometime later, that is the truth."

John felt rage boiling up in him.

MacIver's fingers closed around his son's wrist. "Don't ever try to fight him, Johnny, on my account. You can't win. You can't fight money. All that would happen would be you'd be added to his list of victims and you'd find yourself just where I am."

Two days later ex-Captain Warren MacIver blew his brains out in a Liverpool hotel, and the whole miserable story was raked over again in the press. In his grief John saw that "the truth" was already an indistinct shadow.

Warren MacIver's tragic suicide should have been the end of the saga. It wasn't.

John brought his mother back to America. Moon was living in New York then at the fabulous Hotel Beaumont. John and his mother took a small apartment in Greenwich Village. He had to get a job to support them both. He had no special training except his flying experience in the army. It occurred to him he might land something at one of the big airports or with a commercial airline.

He applied for a job at International. His application required his name, his parents' names and a mass of other detail. As he was leaving the personnel office somebody took a picture of him. In that night's papers there was the picture—not a good one—and a story to the effect that John MacIver, son of a man suspected of passing atomic secrets to the enemy, had applied for a job at International. Once again the old, twisted truth was retold.

It began then for John. His father's story had been hard to credit but now John knew it had been cold, hard truth. He couldn't hold a job. He could never get really started. He demanded to know why. It did no good. Finally he went through the legal maneuver of changing his name. He got a job as a cruise director for the Cunard Line. It took him to London, where he met, among others, Tony Vail—Chambrun's friend. Then one day, for no reason at all, he got the sack. He went to the personnel director, who wasn't a bad guy. Some-one had tipped off the higher-ups that he was Warren MacIver's son. They were sorry, but there were risks of unpleasant publicity.

So it began—an extra in a film, a brief job as counselor at a summer camp for boys, a hassle with unions to get a card that would entitle him to any kind of job. In the middle of this his mother died. It was not unexpected. He had watched her, appalled, for months just seeming to shrivel away. Heart failure, they called it. John knew better. Watching the slow destruction of her husband for seven years had been too much for her; now her son was in the same box. It made life unendurable.

Coming home from his mother's funeral John Wills found himself caught in a new-found habit—talking aloud to himself. He hadn't been thinking of his mother, he realized. He'd been thinking about Aubrey Moon.

"You murdered her!" he said, so loudly that a couple of people on the sidewalk turned to give him a startled look.

Things didn't improve for him. The relentless bad luck, which he knew meant Aubrey Moon, followed him wherever he went. Then one morning he got a registered letter at the rooming house where he was living. It required a return-receipt—to Box 2197 at the General Post Office. He opened the letter and read:

Dear John Wills:

I am well aware of your hatred for Aubrey Moon. I also know the exact state of your finances. I have a proposition that may satisfy your thirst for revenge and your need for money . . .

64

He read on to the end. He would have earned the money if Moon was dead by midnight on February 20th.

It was a joke, of course—a miserable kind of joke. But when, out of curiosity, he went to the Waltham Trust on Madison Avenue the money was there. It was his money. The bank had received a money order with instructions to deposit to the account of John Wills. It was his. No one else could draw it out.

He left it in the bank, but it was like a fever that kept burning him up. He justified taking it in a dozen ways.

The MacIvers had something coming to them after all these years of hell. But if it was due to them, it was due from Moon. The depositor of the money was certainly not Moon. You could look at this proposition, you could walk around it and examine it from all angles like a man thinking of buying a horse, and it would come out only one way. Someone was offering him ten thousand dollars to kill Aubrey Moon.

Each time John Wills came up to this point in his figuring he'd laugh the whole thing off. Whoever his correspondent was, he was nutty as a fruitcake. John was sophisticated enough to know that you could hire yourself a professional assassin in this day and age for a good deal less than ten thousand dollars. Well, he wasn't a professional assassin. Tempting as the money was, lying there in the Waltham Trust waiting for him to take it, he wasn't a killer.

Then, after a bit, the fierce, deep hatred he felt for Aubrey Moon would begin to simmer like a stew on the stove. He would remember the miserable little hotel room in Liverpool where, driven by Moon, Warren MacIver had blown out his brains. He would remember his mother slowly but surely withering away and dying as a result of Moon's relentless persecution of the MacIver clan. He would consider the dead end street

65

in which he found himself, always watched by some agent of Moon's ready to put the skids under him. This man ought to die.

But he wasn't a killer!

He must have read the strange note twenty times a day "I am well aware of your hatred for Aubrey Moon." True, he had probably spilled the whole story a dozen times, when he was high or desperate. Did he know the letter writer? It seemed unlikely. He couldn't think of a single acquaintance who had ten thousand dollars to throw around in this unlikely fashion. Eventually this brought him to a new line of thought.

A man who could do what Moon had done to the MacIvers was quite capable of inflicting the same kind of brutality on other people. John had long ago read everything he could lay hands on about Moon's career. He knew that a lot of important people had been discredited and broken by Moon in his days as a journalist. There were probably many others in a situation comparable to his own. But with ten thousand dollars to throw around? Well, a rich man could be deprived of the things that were essential to him—power, prestige, perhaps even family and the people he loved. A rich man might be as helpless in his frame of reference as John was in his. Then why not do the job himself? It could be a woman, he thought, without the physical courage to do the job. It could be someone ill, unable to get at Moon.

Almost a month of the two months given John Wills by the note writer had passed in this endless walking around the problem. He believed in a society of laws. No one had a right to take punishment into his own hands. You could be arrested, and properly, for destroying a neighbor's dog who bothered you. *But a mad dog?*

Moon, with all his money, could live outside the law.

He had bought a perversion of the truth about Warren MacIver, and the law left him untouched. Moon might be quite unconscious of the fact that he had destroyed John's mother, but he was guilty in her death just the same. He was outside the law, and he could only be punished outside the law.

Almost without his realizing it, John Wills' own moral code, his sense of values, was crumbling. Suppose he took the money? In the end he wouldn't have to go through with it. True, he would be faced with the promised retribution from the letter writer. Moon might die of natural causes in the next month. He was in his seventies. He might be run over by a truck! In the final analysis the decision to take the law into his own hands, John told himself, could wait till the very last day— Moon's birthday. The money would buy him clothes; it could buy him a month without anxiety. He could set himself up at the Beaumont and look over the lay of the land. He could weigh the risk on what would have to be the scene of action.

He went to the Waltham Trust three times and turned away at the door.

The fourth time he went in and withdrew the money.

TWO

The news John Wills had heard over the T.V. had jarred him down to his heels. He had thought of himself as carefully selected by Moon's unknown enemy to do the job. Now here was this Prym girl, hanging herself in despair as time ran out on her, also the recipient of a ten thousand dollar fee. Twenty thousand dollars! The whole thing went out of focus again. It was too bizarre to seem real. Yet his share in it was real enough. The two new suits and the dinner jacket in his closet were evidence. The dozen new shirts in his bureau drawer, concealing the gun and his passport folder, were evidence. The money had been real, hard cash.

He felt as though he was being watched; as though there was a peephole concealed somewhere in the wall of his room. He actually looked for it. Someone very, very rich and very, very loony was back of all this. He could expect almost anything. He looked for a "bug" in the room—a microphone concealed behind a picture or a drape. There was nothing.

He lit a cigarette and stood in the center of the room, trying to rid himself of the sensation that he was being studied by a sinister eye. He had thought of Moon in this position with himself the studying eye. He couldn't make that concept stay put. Obviously someone knew why he was here at the Beaumont. Every move he made would probably be closely watched. He had been victimized for so long by Moon that he found it easy to see himself as being victimized by Moon's enemy. He had a sudden, powerful hunch that if he went through the business of eliminating Moon he would be caught before he took three steps toward safety. He saw himself as little and helpless, like the Prym girl. Someone wanted Moon dead, with a sacrificial goat to hand to the police at the same time.

The money aspect was already completely wild. A man who would spend twenty thousand dollars to buy himself an unlikely killer might well spend more. There might be still another person on stage who had come into a sudden bank account.

John put out his cigarette in the ashtray on the bureau. He had been baited into a trap by the money and by his hatred for Moon. If he killed Moon, an anonymous tip would almost certainly hand him over to the police, no matter how carefully he prearranged a way of escape. If he didn't kill Moon, a rich lunatic would pay him off. "If you take the money," the note said, "and he is not dead by midnight on February 20th, you will not live through the following day yourself."

He made an impatient gesture. It was all far too melodramatic to make sense. And yet the Prym girl had been real and she was dead. Her money had been real and his money was real. He couldn't rid himself of that chill that ran along his spine. He had walked into the plush Beaumont coolly certain that he was in charge of his own destiny. He could go through with it or not. Now he realized that the moment he withdrew the money from the Waltham Trust he had placed himself in the centre of a trap. Heads I lose, tails you win.

So, he told himself, face the cockeyed reality as it is, chum. There is a little time. Tonight, and five more days until midnight on the 20th.

The Trapeze Bar at the Beaumont is suspended in space, like a bird cage, over the foyer to the Grand Ball Room. The foyer, painted a pale chartreuse with a rich cherry wood paneling, is a meeting place for people when the Ball Room itself is not in use. The Trapeze, its walls an elaborate Florentine grillwork, is popular mainly because it is different. An artist of the Calder school has decorated it with mobiles of circus performers, working on trapezes. They sway slightly in the draught from a concealed air-conditioning system. Sitting on a bar stool, sampling an excellent dry martini, John Wills had the feeling that the whole place swayed, which was an illusion.

The feeling that he was being watched had resulted in John's taking special care of his appearance. He had put on his new, very well cut dinner jacket, with a black and gold silk cummerbund and a black and gold tie. Nonchalance, he told himself, should be the keynote. He had to give the appearance to his watcher of scouting the territory with a view to carrying out his end of the bargain, when actually his first concern at the moment was to identify that watcher and find out just what he was up against.

He felt unreal, and the setting supplied by the Beaumont was like something out of a technicolor extravaganza—the green and white striped awning out over the sidewalk, the wall-to-wall green carpeting, the display windows of the best shops in town showing jewels, furs, extravagant women's clothing, the glass chandeliers, the endless mirrors in which he saw himself multiplied a dozen times, the brilliance of the lobby, the cool, shaded intimacy of a half dozen anterooms.

And the people! There was only one person in the lobby, as John made his way from the bank of elevators, who didn't suggest limitless money. That one person spoke to him.

"Mr. Wills?"

"Yes." John felt his muscles tense. Any approach was suspect.

"Jerry Dodd here, sir. House officer. Mr. Chambrun told me to keep an eye out for you."

John relaxed and reached for a cigarette. Dodd was a thin, wiry man in his late forties, John judged, with a professional smile that did nothing to hide the fact that his pale eyes were sharp, penetrating, and able to see and read a great deal in a moment's glance. John had the uncomfortable feeling he might have left a price tag somewhere on his clothes which would tell Jerry Dodd a good deal more than John wanted him to know.

"With all the excitement you've had around here this afternoon," John said, carefully, "I'm surprised Mr. Chambrun remembered me."

"Mr. Chambrun never forgets anything," Dodd said. "Pointed you out to me in the lobby just after lunch. You got the news on your TV set?"

"Yes. Extraordinary business. I'm rather surprised the police made that note public."

Jerry Dodd shook his head. "Had no choice. One of

Mr. Moon's closest buddies is the guy who writes 'Storm Center.' Willard Storm. You know his column?"

"I've read it. Pretty rough stuff from time to time."

"A Grade-A jerk," Jerry Dodd said, cheerfully. "Moon passed on the whole thing to him. The D.A. and the cops had no choice but to make their own statement."

"How did Moon take it?" John asked, lighting his cigarette.

"Not seriously enough to suit us. If I was him I wouldn't laugh it off. Maybe somebody else'll pick up a ten grand offer. I wouldn't like to have anybody tempt me, I don't mind saying." Jerry laughed. "It would be a pleasure."

"I suppose the birthday party Mr. Chambrun told me about will be called off," John said. "I was to cut my teeth on that."

"Oh, the party's on," Dodd said. "Nobody's going to make the Great Man act scared in public. Just making a target of himself, but it's his funeral, not ours. Well, anything I can do to help you, Mr. Wills, just yell."

"Thanks. I have a yen for a good dry martini. Which one of the bars—?"

"The Trapeze. Over there and up one flight. Or you can take the elevator." Dodd laughed. "Avoid the prettiest girls. If they're alone they're pros. The over-dressed, overweight ones are the customers." The pale eyes clouded. "The Prym girl was one of the pros. They'll likely be holding a wake for her up there."

"I'm surprised a place like this tolerates call girls." John said.

"You don't know what 'a place like this' is yet, Mr. Wills. When anything bothers you remember, if the customer wants it and he's willing to pay for it, he can have it. There's only one rule the customer has to obey."

"What's that?"

"He isn't allowed to throw up on the rug in the lobby," Dodd said. "See you, Mr. Wills."

The martini in the Trapeze was perfection. The bartender, a chubby, brown-haired young man, grinned when John offered to pay.

"Just sign this tab, Mr. Wills. It's on the house."

"Come again."

"Mr. Chambrun's orders. Free ride. You're a friend of Tony Vail's, he says. Great guy. He was still here when I first came. Helped me cut my teeth. You in the hotel business, Mr. Wills?"

"Floating hotels," John said, playing his act. "Round the world cruises."

"I wouldn't like that after a while," the bartender said.

"Why?"

"Like seeing a two-character play on Broadway. You know no one unexpected is ever going to show. Sorry, order coming up. I'm Eddie, Mr. Wills. Anything you want, just ask."

Mr. Pierre Chambrun was turning out to be a pleasant surprise. He had evidently bought John's story without any reservations.

John put down his half-full martini glass and lit a fresh cigarette. The Trapeze was doing a rushing business. Two captains moved about among the tables taking orders. Everything was very slick, seemingly unhurried, and yet John saw there was very little time between order and service. Many of the customers were dressed for the evening. The Trapeze was a way station before moving on to a private party somewhere, or one of the hotel dining areas. John had seen the new-rich in action in his time. There was a difference here. As a whole the people in the Trapeze were totally unselfconscious. The women were expensively put together, dressed, jeweled; there were more different hair colors than John could ever remember seeing, and certainly more than God had ever invented. It was hard to put your finger on it. These people were not displaying themselves to a gawking public. Even the recognizable movie star at a corner table seemed relaxed. At the Beaumont she was safe from autograph hunters and glamor-struck adolescents. There were very few young people in the bar.

As the people at the tables turned away from their private conversations for a moment there was a curious blankness to their faces. Eyes rested on John, wondering about him, and passed on without changing expression. He was the self-conscious one. The man, or woman, he was looking for might be sitting out there, calmly studying him. But not one of the social masks he could see had a crack in it. There must be a score of people there, John thought, who could easily afford twenty thousand dollars to have a man killed.

He was just turning back to his martini glass when a woman sat down on the bar stool next to him. She was not dressed for evening. She had on a trench coat and a brown hat with a soft brim that flopped down over her eyes. There were little specks of wet on both the hat and coat, indicating she'd just come in out of a brief snow flurry.

"Eddie!" her voice was unexpectedly loud. She looked around as if she was surprised at its loudness herself.

"Hi, Miss Stewart," Eddie said.

"I would like," the girl said, very precisely, her voice lowered, "a very dry, double vodka martini." She was, John saw, tight as a tick.

"Sure thing, Miss Stewart." Eddie glanced at John and one eyelid dropped. He began to work rapidly with a drink, handling bottles, glass and ice like a magician. In a split second he was stirring the contents of a shaker with a long sliver spoon.

"No games, Eddie!" the girl said sharply.

"How's that?"

"I said no games! That's less than one honest drink!"

"Wouldn't it be better to take 'em one at a time, Miss Stewart?" Eddie asked.

"I said a double and I meant a double, Eddie." Her hand jerked out in an angry gesture and the purse she'd put down on the bar toppled to the floor, spilling out its contents.

Automatically John bent down to pick things up for her. There was quick gratitude in her eyes. There was a bridge of freckles across her nose that somehow made her look like a sad little girl. The stuff that spilled out of her bag was ordinary: a tagged hotel room key, a lipstick, a compact, a small change purse. He put the purse, with its contents restored, on the bar.

"Thank you very much," the girl said.

"You're welcome, Miss Stewart."

Her eyes didn't focus too well as she looked at him. "Who are you? I haven't seen you around here before."

"John Wills," he said. Surely she couldn't be one of the pros Jerry Dodd had mentioned.

"Margo Stewart," she said. "Newspaperman? Detective?"

"Now why should you think I was a detective?" John asked, smiling at her.

"Place is crawling with 'em," she said. "If you're a rich young millionaire you better get out of town—or at least out of the Beaumont. Can you afford ten thousand dollars to get a man murdered, John Wills?"

He felt a faint prickle run along his spine. "I'm a do-it-yourself kid," he said.

Eddie put a new drink down on the bar. He leaned forward. "Miss Stewart is Aubrey Moon's secretary, Mr. Wills," he said. "I guess today kind of shook everyone up who has anything to do with Mr. Moon."

Margo Stewart's vague eyes were still fixed on John.

"You have something to do with Mr. Moon, John Wills?"

"I've been part of his reading public," John said. He put out his cigarette with extraordinary care. "You have had a day."

"You don't know Mr. Moon or you'd know this hasn't been much different from any other day," Margo Stewart said, reaching for her glass. She gulped down half of the double vodka. This was followed by a little spasm, as though she couldn't bear the taste of it.

"People threaten to kill him every day in the week?" John asked, his smile contrived.

"Every day in the week," she said, solemnly. Then she added, surprisingly: "Mostly in the privacy of broken hearts."

"Does your boss have any idea who might have tried to hire the Prym girl?"

She looked up from under the brim of her hat. *"Are* you a newspaperman?"

"Mr. Wills is in the luxury cruise business," Eddie said. He had been unashamedly listening.

"How much would it cost me, John Wills," the girl asked, "to go round the world—and round and round and round forever?"

"About what it costs you now," John said. "I mean, that's what we all do, isn't it? Go round and round and round?"

The girl looked away. "We should let Jack Paar know about him, Eddie. He's a comic."

"You're not laughing," John said. He signaled to Eddie to refill his glass. This accidental meeting with Moon's secretary could be valuable.

She looked at him with the vague eyes. "I know something about you, John Wills, John Wills—" Her voice tapered off.

He felt his muscles growing tense. Here was the old disaster. She was going to place him as Warren Mac-

75

Iver's son—and then Moon would surely know he was here, if he didn't already. Then Chambrun would be told and the game would be up.

"Know something about you," the girl went on, the words thickening. "Can't place it, though. Can't put it in context. Eddie will tell you I spend most of my free time arranging not to be able to put things in context. If you see what I mean? But when I'm sober, John Wills, I'll put you in context." She suddenly sang the children's chant: "You'll be sor—eee!"

"How could I be?" he asked, trying to sound casual. "You can't know anything about me, Miss Stewart. I'm neither famous nor important. Just a glorified boy-guide."

She pointed an unsteady finger at him. "If you're the one who paid that poor little Prym girl to kill my boss I'll put you in context, all right all right. Driving her to what she did was murder, John Wills." Her voice rose. "Why didn't you do your own dirty work?"

"Easy, Miss Stewart," Eddie said. "You're talkin' wild."

"That's me, Eddie," she said. " 'The Call Of The Wild.' " She shook her head. "You don't fit in that context, do you, John Wills? Nice eyes. Nice hands. I like a man's hands. And when I say 'man' I don't mean a lecherous old pervert. I'll buy John Wills that drink, Eddie. Form of apology." She rested her chin on her hand, still looking at John. It was as if she needed to keep her head from tilting forward. "Alcoholic confusion, John Wills. I don't know you from Adam, do I? Whatever I said I don't know you from Adam. You didn't know the Prym girl, did you? Used to visit us once or twice a month. You know what a girl has to put up with when she's paid for it, John Wills? A creeping, hairy spider—with hands going over you like wet suction cups. No, John Wills. I don't know you from Adam. No matter what you do, I don't know you from Adam."

Her chin slipped out of the supporting hand and her head went down on the bar with a resounding thump.

"Boy, is she in the bag," Eddie said. He signaled to one of the dinner-jacketed captains. "I knew she was looping when she came in."

The captain was annoyed. "You shouldn't have served her," he said to Eddie.

"I didn't," Eddie said. "Dash of vermouth and plain water. She asked for a double vodka. I know better than that, Mr. Del Greco. Just thinkin' she had a drink knocked her out, I guess."

"I'm sorry you were annoyed, sir," Mr. Del Greco said to John.

"I wasn't annoyed," John said. "I take it she lives here in the hotel. Could I help get her to her room?"

"Don't bother, sir. It's not a new story." Del Greco signaled a waiter. Almost before John could step aside they'd whisked her out of the bar.

"Service elevator just around the corner," Eddie said. "Isn't the first time we've put her beddy-bys. You know something? Every time she gets tight you catch from her how much she hates Mr. Moon. Wonder why she goes on working for him when she feels that way."

"She's probably very well paid," John said.

But it wasn't that, he told himself. Someone else in the Moon trap. "No matter what you do, I don't know you from Adam." Had she spotted him? Did she guess why he was here? Had she been making a drunken promise to keep still about it?

THREE

It was Tuesday.

John Wills had had his breakfast served in his room.

77

He wanted a chance to go over the collection of morning papers in private. He was in no hurry to move, because at the moment he had no clear notion of where he ought to go or what he ought to do.

The morning papers played the Moon story in a variety of ways. It was difficult, even for the *Times,* to soft-pedal the lurid aspects of the story—the suicide of a known prostitute, admittedly employed by Moon upon occasion, with the strange note in her possession which revealed the existence of a lunatic plot on Moon's life. The *Times* stayed strictly with the facts, quoting the note verbatim. Moon had made no statement to the *Times* man. The police promised the famous author complete protection. The District Attorney's office was investigating the apparent conspiracy against Moon. There was a brief resumé of Moon's career, obviously taken from the paper's morgue. It listed his books and plays, his career as a correspondent in two wars, his literary prizes, his award-winning films. There was no shaft of light on the true character of Moon.

The *Herald Tribune* carried it in much the same way, except for some photographs on an inside page. There was one of Moon posing with an irritated Bernard Shaw. There was another of Moon on the terrace of his villa at Cannes, a glamorous Italian movie star his companion. The third went back to World War I, and showed Moon, uniformed and swagger-sticked, chatting with the handsome Prince of Wales in the streets of a war-torn French village. The fourth was of a dark, beautiful woman with a hairdo of the early twenties. She was described as "Viola Brooke, glamorous star of the British stage, Moon's constant companion in the post-World War I years, whose mysterious disappearance ranks with the famous Judge Crater Case."

The name meant nothing to John Wills. Viola Brooke had disappeared before he was born.

The tabloids had a field day. A team of reporters on the *News* had really done a job. There was a photograph of the dead girl, found in her "lush apartment" where she had "entertained" most of her male customers. "Pamela Prym" had been a stage name. She'd started out as a show girl in Broadway musicals. Her real name had been Maureen O'Connor. She had come out of a mining town in western Pennsylvania. Her father was long since dead in a mine cave-in. Her mother had gone off with a jazz musician and left her child to be cared for by the neighbors. The *News* speculated, with gloves off, on why she had been chosen by Moon's enemy as a possible killer. Why did she "hate" Moon? Moon's biography would not have been recognized by the members of the Noble committee on literature. He had been named in a divorce case; a French cabinet minister had committed suicide, leaving a note to the effect that Moon's articles about him in the press had been too much to bear; the story of Viola Brooke was there, with an account of how she'd walked off stage after the second act of a play in London's West End. When they called her for the third act her dressing room was empty. No one ever saw her again. There was the account of a libel suit against Moon, which he had won. And finally, there it was, the story of Warren MacIver's disgrace and suicide.

John read it with a kind of cold fascination. For the first time in the public prints there was the suggestion that his father might have been telling the truth. The *News* made no bones about its attitude toward Moon. He came out of their account a first-class villain.

The other tabloid carried "Storm Center." Willard Storm had the inside track on all the other reporters as far as Moon was concerned. He was Moon's friend. He had spent most of the day with Moon. He described him as gifted, generous, a victim of the envy of less able men, a fighting journalist in his day who had kept more than one world leader toeing the mark in time of crisis. He described Moon as a brave man. He was, Storm said, in spite of the frightening revelation that someone was prepared to pay a fortune to have him killed, going on with the celebration of his birthday. He had never run in the face of danger. He wouldn't run now. The column ended with a heated warning to the Mayor, the District Attorney, the Police Commissioner and the management of the Beaumont that they were responsible for a "great man's safety." You were left to assume that this warning would have the Mayor, the D.A., the Police Commissioner and Pierre Chambrun trembling in their boots.

John put down the papers and finished his coffee, which was cold. Someone else, not too far away, had read the papers and obviously taken note of the fact that there wasn't even a vague hint or official guess as to who had paid Pamela Prym ten thousand dollars for a job she finally couldn't do. The *News* team had asked another question. "With the Prym girl dead, will Aubrey Moon's enemy try to buy himself a new hatchet man?"

John's mouth was thin and hard as he tied his tie and put on his suit jacket. He had the answer to that question.

The surprising Pierre Chambrun greeted John with easy warmth. "Been waiting for you, Wills."

John found himself looking at the tall, red-haired girl who was perched on the edge of Chambrun's desk. He'd seen her before somewhere.

"Recovered from your bruises?" she asked.

"Bruises?"

"Well, I must say I'm not flattered," Alison said. "Not many young men bounce off me without remembering it."

"Oh God! Yesterday morning," John said. "In the outer office."

Chambrun was at the sideboard, pouring his inevitable cup of Turkish coffee. "Bad beginning, Wills," he said. "This is my Public Relations head, Miss Barnwell. I had planned turning you over to her, but I must admit, if you can meet Alison and not remember her——"

"Let the man up!" Alison said. Her smile was as forthright and friendly as any John could remember. "I remember how I was trembling in my boots out there the first time I came to see you, Mr. Chambrun. I wouldn't have recognized Rock Hudson if he'd bumped into me."

Chambrun came back to his desk, chuckling. "Well, Wills, you walked into a first class melodrama here yesterday."

"I suppose all this hurrah is the worst kind of thing for the hotel," John said, gesturing toward the stack of newspapers on the desk.

Chambrun laughed. "Alison has been distressed by the same thought. It's a standard cliché in the hotel world that scandal hurts business. I've used it myself on occasions. But let me give you the inside truth. Let the word get around that somebody has been poisoned by seafood from your kitchen and your dining rooms will be half empty. Let it be whispered that a mink jacket has been stolen out of one of the rooms by a sneak thief and half your transient guests will depart in a body. A tainted shrimp or the theft of something they can replace ten times over will send them stampeding like cattle in a thunder storm. But let some rich manufacturer of arch supporters shoot his mistress to death on the dance floor in your ballroom and you'll find yourself turning the customers away. A murder, particularly the murder of a celebrity like Moon, would be good for business. I know it and my board of directors know it, no matter how loud their wails and anguished their hand wringings. Publicly we deplore the possibility. Privately we know it's like having a Judy

81

Garland or a Danny Kaye open in your supper club. Good for business."

"That about takes the cake for cynicism," Alison said. She actually sounded shocked.

"What will the hotel do to protect Moon?" John asked.

Chambrun shrugged. "There isn't much we can do. The place is already swarming with cops. He won't let 'em in his apartment, but they're outside in the hall, riding the elevators, wearing out our lobby upholstery. He's covered like a tent. And all the while he's beating his chest and telling the world how unafraid he is. As a matter of fact he's having friends to lunch today in the Grill. We'll need the cops to keep the place from being mobbed."

"I was asking Mr. Chambrun just before you came in, Mr. Wills, how I should deal with the press," Alison said.

"My dear child," Chambrun said, "there is, I believe, a fashion show to be held in the ballroom this afternoon and evening. There is a reception for the Tunisian Ambassador in the Crystal Room. Tomorrow there is a luncheon for the League of Women Voters. Old Mrs. Haven in Penthouse L is having a reception on Thursday at which she will announce a gift of land for a new dog cemetery in Westchester. Those are all items for the Public Relations department, Alison."

"You know I'm asking about Moon," Alison said.

"Moon?" Chambrun said, with elaborate mockery. "Who is Moon? Oh yes, an author who's giving an expensive birthday party here on Saturday night. Mr. Amato can give you a lot of interesting tidbits for your press release on the party. And you've talked to Moon yourself, haven't you?"

"I've talked to him," Alison said, so harshly that John stared at her in surprise. "But you know what I'm asking you, Mr. Chambrun. My office is churning with reporters asking for some kind of statement from the hotel about what's happened and is happening."

"We have no statement to make about Miss Prym's death, beyond a small, sympathetic clucking. We have no statement to make about the threat to Moon. That's for the District Attorney and the police. No statement, Alison." Chambrun smiled, a thin, sardonic smile. "I wonder what the odds are against the Metropolitan Opera Chorus ever getting to sing 'Happy Birthday' on Saturday night? You each want to put a dollar against my two? I'll take the bet either way."

"No matter how much of a heel he is I don't find it funny to joke about his chances of surviving," Alison said.

"You need to develop callouses if you're going to stay in this business, Alison," Chambrun said. He gave her an indulgent, fatherly look. But he was serious. "It's part of our way of life to make a joke about everything. To have feelings about something is to show weakness. Jokes or no jokes, I have feelings. I never knew the Prym girl, but I feel for her. You read what the *News* dug up?"

Alison nodded.

"No chance ever," Chambrun said. "Father dead. No good mother. Probably no formal education. She could only live by showing her body on stage, and after each show geting mauled by every stagedoor John on Broadway. Probably decided if she was going to be mauled she might as well get paid for it. 'Talented body, but with the mind of a small, sentimental child of eight,' Moon said about her. Now I know Moon, Alison—and I suspect you have knowledge of him from the way you reacted a while back. What do you suppose he did to that girl? What kind of degradations did he force on her? Whatever they were she hated him enough, and needed to be free of him enough, to take ten thousand dollars from a mysterious

83

benefactor and decide to kill him. She was at the end of her endurance with Moon. But finally she didn't have the guts to go through with it. A weak girl, you say; a neurotic, disturbed girl. But human—helplessly human. I feel for her. I wish, without having known her, that I could have helped her out of her trouble before it was too late. But Moon?" Chambrun's lips clamped together for an instant. "This is not a human. His whole life has been built around the sheer pleasure of destroying people, hurting them beyond endurance. Read the papers. Miss Prym isn't the first one to commit suicide. There was a French diplomat, probably that British actress, an unfortunate army officer named MacIver who was obviously framed by Moon. Those we know about. How many more over a fifty-year span of calculated sadism? Do you honestly think, Alison, that I give a damn what happens to a man like that? So if I joke about whether they'll get to sing 'Happy Birthday' at his party, it's only to cover up the fact that I secretly hope somebody quietly disembowels him."

"Amen," John heard himself mutter.

"You men!" Alison said.

Chambrun grinned. "As the pacifist said just before the hydrogen bomb lit on his chicken coop. Let Moon worry, let him sweat, and if he dies we'll omit flowers. And I'm not joking. Now Miss Barnwell, take our Mr. Wills out of here and show him how we operate 'the playground of the rich in New York.' "

Alison's office was a three-room suite just down the hall from Chambrun's.

"The first thing we do, Johnny, is get ourselves a table in the Grill for luncheon. I wouldn't want to miss Mr. Moon's first public appearance, would you?"

John shook his head. Like the bird hypnotized by a snake, he thought. Sooner or later he had to see Moon, face to face.

Alison had been right about the press waiting in her office. They had to push their way through a group of men and women clamoring for some sort of news handouts into Alison's private room and close the door.

"I'd like to turn them loose on our Mr. Chambrun for five minutes," Alison said. "He might come up with less comical answers on how to deal with them. Sit down, Johnny." She picked up her phone on the desk. "Jane? Get me Mr. Cardoza in the Grill Room." She glanced at John. "We'll see if my feminine charms are better remembered by Mr. Cardoza than by you! He's the headwaiter in the Grill.—Good morning, Mr. Cardoza? Alison Barnwell here." She covered the mouthpiece with her hand as Mr. Cardoza spoke at length. "I'm not forgotten!" she said. "Now for the big test.—Mr. Cardoza, I want a table for two for today's lunch time.—Yes, I know what's up. Why do you suppose I'd risk my figure eating your extraordinary food?— No, it's not an order from Mr. Chambrun. It's a personal request, dear Mr. Cardoza.—Of course, we'll hang from the chandeliers if necessary.—Bless you, Mr. Cardoza. You're a lamb." Alison put down the phone. "Touch and go," she said. "He's already over-promised himself. Evidently I still have something on the ball."

"You're a very nice girl," John said.

"How faint can your praise be, Johnny?" She laughed. "I guess we've rung all the changes on that gag. But, you see, I noticed you yesterday, which must mean I didn't want to be forgotten. What, exactly, can I do for you, Johnny, as public relations director of this plush-lined aquarium?"

"I'm not sure," John said, avoiding her direct stare. "I don't know enough yet to ask intelligent questions. If I can just tag along with you and see how things work, perhaps in a day or two I'll know exactly what to ask."

"Tag along. Mind if I get personal, Johnny?"

"Of course not," he said, leaving himself wide open.

"I have a nasty kind of mind, Johnny," she said, and somehow the laughter had faded away from her.

"I know better," he said.

"I don't mean nasty-nasty," she said. "Look, I'll put my cards on the table with you, Johnny, because I want you to do the same for me. I was married once upon a time to about the nicest guy there ever was. He was killed in a bomb test out in Nevada. For a while I didn't want to go on living myself. I liked being married. I liked being loved. I knew I wasn't going to fall in love again, and if I did remarry it wasn't going to be the same—not the same at all. Well, I finally picked myself up off the floor and went to work. I had no particular training, but I'd been lucky enough to have a good education. I tried being a lady reporter. I guess I was too much of a lady. It worked around into public relations, for a cruise outfit—like yours, I suppose; a dress designer; a movie company; and finally this. This is where the part about my nasty mind comes in. It's nasty because it remembers odd things. After I first saw you yesterday it remembered something it should have forgotten."

"Oh?"

"The picture of a young man walking out of the personnel office at International Airport. This young man's father had been a bomb expert. Because of my association with bombs, perhaps, it stuck. The story that went with the picture stuck—the story about an unhappy man who killed himself after an encounter with Aubrey Moon."

John drew a deep breath. "You know who I am," he said.

"Yes, I know, Johnny." Her smile was gentle. "I

86

thought I ought to tell you if we're going to spend time together for the next few days. Do you know that when Mr. Chambrun mentioned your father you turned white as a sheet back there in his office? Mr. Chambrun didn't notice. He was too fascinated by the sound of his own words."

"You didn't tell him what you knew?"

"Why should I? As I recall the story you'd legally changed your name. Reminding people that you'd once been John MacIver was what was giving you trouble, wasn't it?"

"So much trouble."

"One thing bothers me, Johnny. When you came here to find out about the hotel business you must have known that Aubrey Moon lived here."

"I knew."

"Will he recognize you if he sees you?"

"I don't know."

"One thing you can count on. Mr. Chambrun won't kick you out on your ear just because Moon asks him to. Johnny?"

"Yes?"

"Johnny, my nasty mind again. Are you really here to find out about the hotel business, or does it have something to do with Moon?"

His mouth felt dry. It was too late to pretend with her. She'd caught him with his guard completely down.

"That mind of yours is nastily persistent," he said, trying to smile.

She was silent for a moment. "Would you like to give me a chance to understand your side of it, Johnny?" she asked, quietly.

He sat there, looking down at his hands which were tightly folded in front of him. Nice hands, the Stewart girl had said last night. Almost certainly the Stewart girl had known who he was, too. "No matter what you do I don't know you from Adam."

He looked up at Alison and felt a strange ache in his throat. He remembered that same ache when, as a kid, he had fought back tears for some reason. He was aware of a terrible urgency to tell her the whole story, every detail of it. Since the day of his father's death he'd never been able to say it all to anyone. It had been too painful for his mother to share with him. Not once in twelve years had he been able to explain the deep sense of loss his father's suicide had brought to him. He'd really had no father. First the war, and then the persecution by Moon which had turned his father into a hopeless, defeated stranger. There had been no one with whom he could share his own defeats. There had been no one to hang on to when he felt his own moral code crumbling. There had been no one to hear him wake from a troubled sleep, crying out wild threats of revenge against Moon. It was boiling up in him now as he looked into Alison Barnwell's troubled blue eyes.

He moistened his lips. "I came here more than half intending to kill him," he said. And then it tumbled out of him, the whole grim story. The saga of his father, doomed by Moon's sadistic hatred; the slow wasting away of his mother; his own unbearable frustrations. Alison never interrupted once in the telling. He believed that what he saw in her face was sympathy—or at least pity.

"It wouldn't have taken much at any time," he said. "If I'd found myself standing next to him in a subway station I could have pushed him down on the tracks and felt almost no guilt. I hadn't come to the point where I could go out hunting for him, but if the chance had come my way I'd have taken it, I think. Then five weeks ago the note came."

"Note?" It was Alison's first question.

"Up in my room I have an exact duplicate of the

note they found in Pamela Prym's purse. Except mine is addressed to me."

"Johnny!"

"The money was there in the Waltham Trust. I—I let it stay there. All the time that I kept telling myself I was a civilized human being who wouldn't kill another man, even though I hated him, I remembered the money was there. Finally—finally I went and drew it out. I bought some clothes. I got in touch with Tony Vail in London and had him write a note of introduction to Chambrun. I thought—I don't know what I thought. I'd just scout out the situation. I didn't have to go through with it. But—I bought a gun. Then, with everything nicely arranged and a week in which to make my decisions, the lid is blown off by the Prym girl's suicide. There is someone—someone mad as a hatter—determined to end Moon's career not later than his seventy-fifth birthday party on Saturday. He thought the Prym girl might do it for him. He thinks I may do it for him. He may even have other strings to his bow. He is someone who knows all about me; who obviously knew all about the Prym girl. If he's crazy enough to carry out this scheme, he's crazy enough to carry out the threats he made in the note. I will not live through Sunday, he promised me, if I take the money and don't go through with it."

"So you went off the rails for a minute," Alison said, in a practical voice. "You took the money. You've spent some of it. But you're not going through with it. So you go to the police, hand over your copy of the note, and cooperate with them in finding this lunatic."

"You're a doll for listening," he said, fumbling for a cigarette.

"Well, isn't that what you're going to do?" she demanded.

"I haven't thought it out," he said.

"What's to think?" She sounded impatient. "My dear

89

Johnny, don't behave like a character in a bad detective story who doesn't do the obvious thing to protect himself. So you took money to kill a man, which probably puts you behind some kind of legal eight ball. But your story's real, Johnny. If you go to this Lieutenant Hardy, show him the note, turn over your gun, offer to help—surely they'll give you some kind of a break."

"How could I help them?"

"Just giving them your copy of the note is help! It'll show them that Moon is in greater danger than they may think."

"So I'll be helping to protect Moon," he said, a bitter little smile on his lips.

"Johnny, Johnny, Johnny! You'll be helping yourself! You've allowed yourself to live like a character in a melodrama for a dozen years. You've got to stop it! You've got to talk to people like you've talked to me. You've got to get help, instead of standing still in the center of space and acting as a whipping boy for Moon. Now you be a big boy, Johnny. You go up to your room and get that note—and your gun—and bring them both back down here. Hardy's somewhere in the hotel. I'll have him here when you get back."

John stood up. He felt as if a great mountain had been lifted off him. She was such a down-to-earth, common-sense kind of girl.

"Do you always play the role of Mother Confessor, Alison?" he asked.

"When you start thinking of me as a 'mother,' my buck-oh, you can get out of this office and stay out of it!" Her smile warmed him down to his heels. "Bless you, Johnny. You know this is right for you, don't you?"

Lieutenant Hardy listened like a man who didn't believe a single word of what he was hearing. From time to time, as John Wills talked, he looked down at the note which John had given him at the start of their conversation. Then he would glance at the gun which rested on the edge of Alison's desk.

John's story finally came to an end.

"It's the most unreasonable, unlikely, cockeyedest story I've ever listened to," Hardy said. He gave Alison a suspicious look. "This isn't some kind of a publicity build up, is it, Miss Barnwell?" But he knew it wasn't. He'd held the note up to the light and saw it was the same grade of paper—same watermark—as the one found in the Prym girl's purse. He'd been a cop pounding a beat on Broadway when the papers had been carrying the story of Warren MacIver's court-martial. If Wills was a phony he wouldn't pick a story with which it would be so easy to check his connection. No, wild as it sounded, this young Mr. Wills was telling the truth.

"I daresay it'll check out," Hardy said. "The bank—the whole, screwball business." He glared at John. "Who else knows the score?"

"Only Miss Barnwell," John said.

"Conspiracy to commit a homicide is the charge they can bring against you," Hardy said. And when nobody commented on this he got up and began to prowl Alison's office. "You think these notes—and the threats in 'em—are on the level, Wills?"

"If you were in my shoes would you want to run the risk that they aren't?" John asked.

Hardy sighed. "We got no choice, do we? What's needed on this case is a headshrinker, not a detective. How an apparently sensible guy like you could wander around town for five weeks trying to make up your mind whether to take that dough and kill a man is beyond me. Surely you must have realized you were being set up as a pigeon! A guy who'll spend that kind of money on a scheme is going to make damn sure the job gets done. You and the Prym girl and maybe some other characters are set up to hold the bag. Where do we look for this creep? So we go to the General Post Office and check out that box where your return receipt went. How do they know who hired the box? Somebody paid for it and used it—and if the guy didn't want to be recognized he won't be recognized!"

"It's been my theory he'd be here in the hotel," John said. "He'd want to watch—me and others. If you're running a marionette show you have to be around to pull the strings."

"How bad do you want to see this guy caught?"

John glanced at Alison. "I want to live beyond Saturday night, if that's what you're asking."

"Maybe you got guts," Hardy said. "You came here halfway prepared to kill a guy. You ready to buy some life insurance by running some risks?"

"What kind of risks?"

"How do I know?" Hardy exploded. "This is loony-ville! There aren't any handles to this case—with Moon up there in his damn Chinese boudoir, smiling like a Siamese cat and daring us to protect him! Maybe we ought to take you and your note up there and say 'Look, buddy, the gun is really loaded!' " Hardy's eyes narrowed. "And maybe not." He glared at Alison. "How good are you at keeping your mouth shut, Miss Barnwell?"

"As good as you want me to be, Lieutenant."

"Okay. Suppose we play it like nothing has happened. You haven't talked to me. You haven't talked to anyone, Wills. You're still what you were when you got up this morning—a maybe-killer. You're scouting out the lay of the land, pretending to learn the luxury hotel business. Nobody knows about the note. Nobody knows about the money. Maybe this guy will tip his hand—wink too broad an eye. Maybe he'll want to remind you time is running out. He speaks to you at a bar. He calls you on your room phone. He slides a note under your door. Some contact. Maybe we get a lead. Just maybe.

And maybe we outsmart ourselves and somebody shoves you down an elevator shaft. A guy who can know so much about your life, Wills, and the Prym girl's life, may also know that we're sitting here right now sewing up a shroud." He glanced down at the intercom system on Alison's desk. It was turned off.

"You'd probably catch him after you'd scraped me off the bottom of the shaft," John said.

"If I could guarantee that I might make you run the risk," Hardy said, "instead of asking you to volunteer."

John looked at Alison. She was frightened, he saw. It made his heart beat a little faster. It mattered to her what happened to him.

"I'll play it your way," he told Hardy.

PART 3

THERE IS considerable difference between the discussion of a plan, over a cigarette and in the privacy of a pleasant place like Alison's office, and putting that plan into action. It is one thing to say "Yes, I will be the cheese in the trap," and quite another actually becoming the cheese.

John Wills was not a physical coward, but the persecuted life he'd lived for the last twelve years had turned him into a defeatist as far as his own future was concerned. He had come to accept the fact that there was no way for him to win in his long struggle with Moon and Moon's world. Now, in the space of an hour, two things had happened to him. In Alison he had found an escape hatch for emotions that had been bottled up in him to the bursting point—to the bursting point where he'd actually considered killing a man. In Hardy he had found an ally who offered him a gambling chance to free himself of the whole mess. A faint flicker of hope began to burn, like a candle in a distant window.

Hardy had left him alone with Alison. The lieutenant was going to organize his special surveillance of John. There would be two or three men whose job it was to watch John and everyone who seemed interested in him or approached him in public. These detectives, plus

Jerry Dodd's hotel security staff, would be on constant watch. In fifteen minutes they would all be in the lobby where Hardy would point them out to John as he and Alison went to the Grill for lunch.

"You've got to know who's on your team and who isn't," Hardy said. "We don't want you wasting your time wondering about one of my boys."

The lieutenant was adamant on another point. No one, but no one, was to know what they were up to. Alison had felt an obligation to alert Mr. Chambrun.

"You've got to be treated by everyone you contact in a perfectly natural fashion," Hardy said. "We have no idea where there may be a leak. A guy who will toss around twenty thousand bucks the way our friend has can bribe too damned high for comfort. A bellman, a telephone operator, a housemaid—if there's even a whisper that you aren't what our friend thinks you are, his potential hired hand, we're up the creek."

"You don't trust Mr. Chambrun?" Alison asked.

"I don't trust anyone to behave naturally if they're in on this. I don't trust you, Miss Barnwell, but I can't help myself! Our one hope, Wills, is that our friend thinks you still haven't made up your mind and that you need a little pushing, a little urging, a little warning. That's how we'll get him—if we do get him."

"I'm not sure how well I can act the part with a target painted in the middle of my back," John said.

"The target's been there all along," Hardy said. "You only just got wise to it is- all. If you act a little nervous and uncertain so much the better. He'll think you're still trying to make a decision."

So Hardy went off to alert his men. Alison looked at John, her lovely face a picture of anxiety.

"Oh, Johnny, what have I gotten you into?"

"Dear Alison," he said. He wanted to go to her, but he stayed where he was, standing across her desk from her. "I remember my father saying something when I was a kid. I was ten years old and my mother and I were being evacuated from London back here to the States for the duration. My father said it to me, but I realized he meant it for my mother. 'Someday, Johnny,' he said, 'you'll find out that no man is whole by himself. He's like a pound note torn in half—not worth anything unless you have the matching piece. I'll never be whole again, Johnny, until you bring the matching piece back to me.' He meant my mother, of course. I—I've never had a matching piece, Alison. I know you've only helped me because you're a nice girl, with a big, warm heart. I know I'm not your matching piece. But for a little while here you've made me feel whole by sharing my problem with me. Thank you—very, very much."

"There's not much I can say to that, is there?" she said, gravely. "If it's helped, I'm happy. I know what it's like, with the matching piece gone for keeps."

John knew he'd have to keep remembering that. Alison could offer friendship, but that was all.

Exactly fifteen minutes after Hardy's departure they went down to the lobby together. The Beaumont was buzzing. How it had got out that Aubrey Moon meant to make an appearance for lunch John couldn't guess. Perhaps through his columnist friend, Willard Storm. There was a mob outside the entrance to the Grill trying to get at Mr. Cardoza, the captain, who stood on the other side of a red velvet rope, apologizing over and over for the fact that there wasn't a table or an inch of space unreserved.

Dutifully John looked around the crowded lobby for Hardy. The lieutenant was talking to a heavy-set man near the newsstand. For an instant his eye caught John's, but without a flicker of recognition. As it did he put his hand on the heavy-set man's shoulder. Then he walked away to the other side of the lobby. A tall thin man was looking in one of the display windows. Once more Hardy's hand rested on a shoulder. This maneuver was repeated twice more. After the fourth man had been identified, the lieutenant glanced at John once more and then disappeared in the direction of the elevators.

"Oh, Lord!" Alison said, softly.

John turned and saw her watching the approach of a strange old woman. Her hat looked like a fruit vendor's stand, covered with floating veils. Her mink coat shone in the bright lights from the chandeliers and fitted her like an oversize tent. Cuddled in her arms was a black and white Japanese spaniel.

" 'The Madwoman Of Chaillot,' " Alison said. "She has the penthouse next to Moon's. Mrs George Haven."

"The one who's interested in dog cemeteries?"

"The one! Be nice to her, Johnny, and for heaven's sake speak to Toto!" It was all the warning Alison had time to give.

Mrs. Haven bore down on them like a schooner under full sail. "Well, Barnwell!" she said. Her voice was like the booming of ancient guns. People turned to look—and kept looking. She was a museum piece.

"Good morning, Mrs. Haven," Alison said. "And how is dear little Toto today?" It didn't sound like Alison.

"Annoyed with me," Mrs. Haven said. "I didn't give him anything but a functional walk. He expects the Park at this time of day." Glassy eyes fixed on John. "And who is this, Barnwell?"

"John Wills—Mrs. Haven," Alison said.

"How do you do, Mrs. Haven," John said. He reached out and touched the spaniel's flat head. "Hello, old man." The spaniel gave him a complacent smirk.

"I'd expected you before this to talk about my luncheon on Thursday, Barnwell. When do you expect to put out any publicity about the new cemetery?"

"Could I come up tomorrow morning?"

"If you can get there!" Mrs. Haven said. She looked

around her, a fur-wrapped picture of indignation. "This absurd Moon man and his troubles. I can't get to my own front door without becoming embroiled with half the Manhattan police force. If he's going to get himself murdered he should do it less publicly. Will ten o'clock tomorrow do, Barnwell?"

"Perfectly, Mrs. Haven."

Mrs. Haven fixed the deep glassy eyes on John again. "You can't be all bad, Wills," she said.

"I hope not!" John said.

"Spoke to Toto. I always say people who like dogs can't be all bad. You shall come to tea some afternoon."

"It would be a pleasure," John said.

"That remains to be seen. Ten o'clock, Barnwell." And off she went, sails filled again, toward the elevators.

"Wow!" Alison said.

"Thanks for the tip about Toto!"

Alison laughed. "She bought her penthouse here about seven months ago, and she's never yet spoken a word to Mr. Chambrun. It bothers him. He's the only member of the staff who isn't in on the joke. Love me, love my dog. You see, he's never gotten around to speaking to Toto! Well, we'd better get to our table if Mr. Cardoza's to keep if for us. You any good at the flying wedge?"

They elbowed their way through the crowd to the velvet rope. Mr. Cardoza, cool as ice, let them through. The people outside the rope eyed them as though they were villains.

"I shall expect at least an evening at the theatre for this, Miss Barnwell," Mr. Cardoza said to Alison as he led them toward a table in the already filled room.

"It's a date," Alison said. "I didn't realize what I was asking, Mr. Cardoza."

The captain pulled out her chair for her, smiling

blandly. "I always knew he had two heads," he said. "I don't think you're likely to be hit by any stray bullets here."

"You don't really think—?"

"I don't," Mr. Cardoza said. "I don't think he would come if it was dangerous. If you'll excuse me—"

They were hardly settled at the table when they heard voices rising in an excited buzz. The Great Man was crossing the lobby. A moment later he appeared at Mr. Cardoza's velvet rope.

It was one of the few times John Wills had ever seen him in the flesh. He felt his muscles grow tense and his jaws clamp tightly together. Then Alison's cool hand covered his.

"Easy, Johnny," she said.

Moon stood in the doorway, looking around the room with a supercilious eye. He wore a charcoal gray suit, perfectly tailored, a black and white Tattersall vest, a jaunty bow tie. He could easily have been a dissipated fifty instead of his acknowledged seventy-five years. His left hand smoothed the little black mustache. His right was in his trouser pocket, casually jingling coins. He didn't speak, but you could almost hear him thinking: "All right, suckers, have a good look."

John turned away. The vision of his father's tortured face had come back to him and he could hear Warren MacIver's tired, bitter voice. "I didn't realize I'd made an enemy who had the power, the influence, and above all the money, to hold me down until I was dead—or he was dead."

"The one who looks like an innocent college sophomore is Willard Storm, the columnist," John heard Alison say.

He brought himself to look back at the entrance. Mr. Cardoza was bowing Moon to a table. Directly behind Moon was a young man in shell-rimmed glasses, very Madison Avenue.

"Birds of a feather," Alison said. "In his own way Master Storm is a modern version of Aubrey in his youth."

The two men came down to the table reserved for them in the center of the room. Mr. Cardoza hovered over them. John got a glimpse of Chambrun in the entrance with Hardy and a couple of his men flanking him. Moon was being carefully watched. A photographer was being forcibly escorted away from the entrance by Jerry Dodd and another house officer.

"Mr. Chambrun won't allow any kind of a side show, no matter how much Moon may like it," Alison said.

At that moment Moon's little dark eyes spotted Alison. He bowed, giving her a mocking smile. Color rose in Alison's cheeks. John was about to make an angry comment when he realized that Moon was studying him. The smile had faded. The black eyes had narrowed to two, puffy slits. Then Moon turned and spoke to Willard Storm. Instantly the columnist turned his black rimmed glasses on John.

"I think he's spotted me," John said.

"It's a free country," Alison said, angry at herself for blushing.

John waited for something to happen, but Moon had turned to a discussion of the luncheon menu with Mr. Cardoza. Storm had taken a notebook from his pocket. He wrote something in it, glancing up once in the process at John.

"Miss Barnwell?"

John glanced up at the man who'd stopped by their table. He'd been handsome at one time in his life, John thought. The profile was still good. He wore a black coat and striped trousers and carried a folder with papers in it under one arm.

"Mr. Amato! Hello!" Alison said. "This is John Wills—Mr. Amato, our banquet manager."

Amato bowed. "I've heard about you, Mr. Wills, from Chambrun. He tells me you're interested in a luxury operation." He turned his head to glance at Moon. "You might think he was the current Hamlet the way he plays it." Amato shuddered slightly. "This may not be the moment, Miss Barnwell, but Chambrun said you might be interested in the details for Saturday night. May I join you?"

"Of course," Alison said.

Amato sat down in an extra chair. He opened the folder he was carrying. "I have the menu here. You might be able to use some of the details in your releases."

"Happy birthday!" Alison said, smiling at the man.

Little beads of sweat appeared on Amato's forehead. "Damn him!" he said, softly.

"It can't be that bad, Mr. Amato."

"It will be ten times worse than you can imagine," Amato said. "With all this excitement, all this hullabaloo, the party will be a matter of national—you might say, world-wide—interest. That means His Majesty will make things twenty times more difficult. In the spotlight he is a fiend. I dreamed he might be persuaded by the police to give up the whole thing."

"They tried," Alison said. "The spotlight is just what our Mr. Moon wants."

"Oh, God!" Amato said. He took a linen handkerchief out of his breast pocket and wiped his forehead.

"But Mr. Amato, all you have to do is choose the right foods and wines. That's your business, and Mr. Chambrun tells me you're the best there is at it."

"You don't understand," Amato said. "It's impossible to please him. And it's more than food and wine." The glance he gave the center table was venomous. "It's stop-watch precision. The hors d'oeuvres at precisely eight, not a minute one way or the other. Plates to be removed exactly six minutes later. A signal to one of the orchestras to play so that the noise of the removal of dishes will be covered. Soup exactly six minutes later. And so on and so on."

"So you present him with your menu, he makes his changes, and you rent yourself a stop watch," Alison said, cheerfully. "Once you've started there's nothing you can do about it if your timing is off on some routine. You have the menu there, Mr. Amato."

Amato nodded, wiping his face again.

"I'm dying to know how a man spends thirty thousand dollars on a dinner for his friends," Alison said.

"That's not a real figure, is it?" John asked. "Mr. Chambrun mentioned it, but I thought he was just exaggerating to make a point."

"It will be more," Amato said, "including the gifts—the bar service in the ballroom foyer, the Metropolitan Opera Ensemble." He opened the folder and took out several Verifaxed sheets of paper, handing one to each. John found himself studying the menu with a kind of awe.

GRAND BALL ROOM AND SUITES 1–2
INVITATIONS 7 P.M.
SERVICE   8 P.M.
ABOUT 250 GUESTS

In Charge: Mr. Amato

AN EXCELLENT ASSORTMENT OF COLD CANAPES TO CONSIST OF:

Brioche au Caviar
Cornet of Smoked Salmon with Horseradish Sauce
Stuffed Eggs with Creamed Anchovies
Stuffed Celery
Prosciutto on Grissini

HOT HORS D'OEUVRES FROM ROLLING SIL-VER CHAFING DISH TO INCLUDE:

Escargot Provençal
Crab meat Remick
Barquettes of Mushrooms

MENU	WINES
KANGAROO TAIL SOUP	Madeira, Special
LA CRUSTADE FEUILLETEE AUX QUENNELLES CARDINAL DE MER	Gewurstraminer, Reserve Exceptionelle
Brillat Savarin	Domaine Nugel 1963
POLENTA E CONIGLIO PIEMONTESSE	Volnay, Clos des Chenes, Domaine A. Rapiteau-Mignon 1953
ROAST VENISON GRAN VENEUR	Chambolle Musigny, Ior Cru
Artichoke Bottoms with Purée of Chestnuts	Domaine Jules Regnier 1952
QUESO Y SALADE CAMPESINO	
Con Pimientos	
DESERT MOON	St. Marceaux
PETIT FOURS	Extra Quality Brut, Magnums
DEMITASSE	Liqueurs Dubouche Bisquit Fockink Kummel

With the arrival of DESERT MOON "Happy Birthday" will be sung as a group number with two orchestras and the entire Metropolitan Opera Ensemble.

Sandwiches and Champagne will be served in the foyer for those guests who linger after the dinner is completed.

Room Rent	$5,000
Beverages and cocktails	3,168
Wines	2,177
Food, 250 Covers @ $30.00	7,500
Sandwiches 200 @ $1.00	200
Champagne 75 bottles @ $12.00	900
Total	$18,945
Gratuities	2,841.75
Gratuities to captains, etc. (Est.)	600.
Grand Total	$22,386.75

"Of course," Mr. Amato said, wiping his face, "when you add the cost of two orchestras, the Metropolitan Ensemble, and gold lighters and compacts for all the guests, thirty thousand won't come close to covering it. And I have forgotten the flowers from Hawaii—at least three thousand dollars, cigars from Sumatra, cigarettes with Mr. Moon's initials on them, hand-painted menus at five dollars apiece. Oh, thirty thousand is way under!"

"You have arranged this menu and arrived at these estimates since ten o'clock yesterday morning?" John asked.

Amato shrugged. "My job." He was pleased at having impressed. "But persuading Mr. Moon to okay it is another matter."

"Have you ever thought of running for President of the United States, Mr. Amato?" John asked. "The executive ability, the grasp of figures—" He shook his head. "I'll campaign for you."

"Dear Mr. Amato," Alison said, "what is 'Desert Moon'?"

"It is a birthday cake, but rather special," Amato

107

said, obviously pleased. "It will be constructed in the shape of Mr. Moon's yacht, the *Narcissa*. Dry ice, concealed in a container in the center of the cake, will cause smoke to come out of the funnel. The portholes will be illuminated by small flashlight bulbs. It will, if I say so, be a work of art."

"And as the Great Man cuts into it," Alison said, a note of awe in her voice, "the chorus of the Metropolitan Opera will sing—"

" 'Happy Birthday,' " Amato said.

Mr. Cardoza, smooth and noiseless, had approached them. "Yes indeed. Happy Birthday," he said under his breath. "You are summoned into the Presence, Amato."

"What?" Amato seemed to jump in his chair.

"You have been seen. You are wanted. Before publicity is issued on the menu he may want to make some changes after all. You, Miss Barnwell, will be good enough to accompany Amato and join the Great Man in a pre-luncheon cocktail. He wants no publicity until he has given his final approval. *Allons, mes enfants!*"

"Sorry, Johnny," Alison said.

John watched Alison and the sweating Amato go over to Moon's table. It was a nice little scene, from the point of view of the curious public. Moon played it with elegance and charm, rising from his chair, taking Alison's reluctant hand, raising it to his lips, and then guiding her around the table to a chair provided by Mr. Cardoza.

There was no chair for Mr. Amato. He stood, like a guilty schoolboy, waiting for Moon to get around to him. Moon was in no hurry. He was the center of attention, and Alison was a beautiful girl. The whole thing was a little too much for the dead-pan faces John had seen in the Trapeze Bar the night before. They made no bones about their fascination with Moon.

It provided John with an opportunity to look around the room, searching for that one person who might be watching him, wondering about his reaction. So far as he could tell, not a soul in the Grill was paying the slightest attention to anyone but the Great Man.

Before the agonized Mr. Amato got his turn, there was a further interruption. Margo Stewart appeared in the entrance, was passed through the velvet rope by Mr. Cardoza's assistant. She headed straight for Moon's table, looking neither right nor left. She was wearing that "good black dress" that every business girl has in her wardrobe. John only had a side view of her, but he felt certain she must be feeling like hell after last night.

At the table Margo handed Moon a slip of paper. He glanced at her as though the sight of her made him ill. You could almost see the faint shudder of distaste. The interruption broke the spell he was creating with his interpretation of the role of an elderly but gallant Don Juan. He glanced at the slip, made an impatient gesture of dismissal, and turned attentively back to Alison.

Margo Stewart made her exit a different way. She came straight down a side alley between tables that brought her past John at his table. She looked at him as though he was a decoration on the wall. There was no sign of her ever having laid eyes on him before. Maybe she had no memory of last night, John thought. She had really been stoned. Then, as she passed the table she brushed against him.

She was gone, but in John's lap was a small, crumpled piece of paper. He looked quickly at Moon's table. Neither Moon nor Willard Storm had paid any attention to Margo's exit. Moon was apparently giving a cocktail order to Mr. Cardoza. Storm was having his moment to be charming to Alison.

Without lifting the paper into sight John unfolded it.

May I please see you! Don't call the Penthouse.
M.S.

John turned slowly to look at the entrance. Margo Stewart had already disappeared through the crowd outside the velvet rope.

Back at Moon's table the Great Man had finally condescended to recognize Mr. Amato. From the curl of his lip as he spoke to the banquet manager it was easy to guess a verbal lashing was in progress. Amato's face went from beet-red to the color of ashes. With unsteady hands he handed copies of the menu to Moon and Storm. At which precise moment Pierre Chambrun materialized from somewhere, suave, smiling, unperturbed, to post himself beside his banquet manager. Although he continued to stand rigidly erect you could almost feel Amato leaning on Chambrun for support.

It was like watching a silent movie without subtitles. Moon said something sharp and angry to Chambrun. Chambrun replied, smiling. Moon went into a second tirade of some sort. Suddenly he was gesturing toward John. Storm and Alison turned to look at John, but Chambrun listened without a vestige of concern. When Moon had exhausted himself, Chambrun said something to Amato and then to Alison. Amato literally ran from the Presence, leaving his folder of papers with Chambrun. Alison got up from her chair, said something polite to Moon, and came swiftly back across the room to John. Moon, white with anger, was chewing out an unimpressed Pierre Chambrun as Alison reached the table and sat down beside John.

"That blessed man!" she said.

Almost instantly Mr. Cardoza appeared with two martinis they hadn't ordered.

"Doubles, Miss Barnwell," he said, cheerfully. "On me! Our Mr. Chambrun is quite a boy, no?"

"Yes!" Alison said. She turned to John. "Mr. Cardoza

will forgive us, I know, if we have his drink and then go somewhere else for a sandwich, Johnny. I don't think I could go on breathing in here!"

"By all means," Mr. Cardoza said. "I'll have a waiter serve the drinks up in your office if you like, Miss Barnwell." He gave them a wry smile. "There's a couple behind the rope there waving a twenty dollar bill under my nose for a table. I'd even make a profit."

Alison's hand on Cardoza's arm was all the thanks he needed. She got up and walked quickly toward the entrance. John followed. Out of the corner of his eye he saw Moon still berating Chambrun, who looked as though he might actually be enjoying it.

They pushed through the crowd outside the rope. There was actually no chance to talk until they'd reached the fourth floor and started down the corridor to Alison's office.

"Moon is something you wouldn't believe!" Alison said, her voice angry. "He can't look at you without its being an insult. He managed, somehow, in front of Storm and Amato, to make it seem as though he and I shared some kind of secret. I'm sure Storm thinks I spend my spare time romancing that creep!"

She barged through the anteroom of her office and into her private room.

"Shut the door, Johnny!"

John shut the door. Alison stood by her desk, back to him. For a moment he thought she was going to burst into tears. Instead she brought both fists down on her desk.

"That slimy bastard!" she said. Finally she straightened up and turned to face him. "Sorry, Johnny."

He grinned at her. "Have a second helping, if you like."

"Johnny, there's trouble."

"Moon recognized me," he said, his mouth hardening.

111

"Recognized you, told Storm exactly who you are, chided me for having lunch with his 'enemy.' Finally he accused Chambrun of harboring a potential murderer in his hotel."

"And Chambrun?"

"He knows who you are, Johnny. If he didn't he put on a wonderful act. He is a doll! Where did he come from, Johnny? Just suddenly he was there. What Moon was doing to Amato shouldn't happen to a dog. And there was Chambrun! 'For such an important occasion as your birthday, Mr. Moon,' he said, smooth as oil, 'I don't choose to leave the details to my subordinates. Run along, Amato.' "

"And did he run!"

" 'I will also convey your wishes to Miss Barnwell about publicity,' Chambrun went on. 'We mustn't keep her from her luncheon guest.' 'Who may well be the killer you people are alleged to be protecting me from!' Moon shouted at him. 'Do you know who he is?' I was too stunned to try to stop it, Johnny. But Chambrun was way ahead of me. 'He is John Wills,' he said. 'Learning the hotel business. He is the son of a man who blew out his brains on your account.' 'And you give him the run of the hotel?' Moon said, 'when you know someone's trying to kill me?' 'Is there any rule that says only people who love you may be admitted to the Beaumont, Mr. Moon?' " Alison was breathing hard, as if she'd been running. "I got out of there then, Johnny."

There was a knock on the office door.

"Probably our drinks," Alison said. "I hope Mr. Cardoza thought to keep them doubles."

John opened the door and stood gaping. Chambrun, a napkin draped over his arm, stood there with three drinks on a tray and a hot chafing dish of canapes.

"May I serve you in here, sir?" Chambrun asked, his eyes dancing. With mock formality he brought in the

112

tray and set it down on Alison's desk. He handed a glass to Alison, bowing, and waved to John. "Help yourself, sir." He dropped the act. "Quite a little clambake," he said. He picked up his own glass. "Here's to weeding out the sheep from the goats. And when I say 'goat' I refer to your would-be admirer, Alison," He took a sip of his drink. "Yes, I know who you are, John Wills."

Well, that was that, John thought.

Chambrun took a silver case out of his pocket and removed one of his Egyptian cigarettes. John, his hand not too steady, held his lighter for him. Chambrun's dark eyes squinted through the smoke at him.

"Lesson in the hotel business for both of you," he said. He lifted the lid of the chafing dish. The dish was divided into sections which contained small fish cakes, cocktail sausages, and stuffed, deviled clams. Alison shook her head as he offered it. He selected a fish cake on a toothpick for himself. "You can't handle my kind of job, children, without knowing everything you're supposed to know and a great deal you're not supposed to know. Aubrey Moon is a cross I have to bear. To bear it successfully I need to know everything I can about it. It isn't safe for our Mr. Moon to be able to surprise you. It sometimes takes a little while for my mental filing system to work efficiently. But a few minutes after my first interview with you, John, I placed you. You are the son of the late Warren MacIver. Naturally I wondered at once whether your story about learning the hotel business was true."

"It isn't," John said. "I—"

Chambrun silenced him with a gentle gesture. "I decided it might be, and I certainly wasn't going to make things any harder for you than they'd been. Then, today, I decided I'd been wrong when I knew that you and Alison and Lieutenant Hardy had been cooking up some scheme among you."

113

"You know that?" Alison asked, in a small voice.

"When I don't know what's going on in my own hotel I'll have to retire," Chambrun said. "Don't ask me how I know. This much must be obvious to you. There are people on my staff I can trust one hundred percent." He gave Alison a sly little smile.

"I'm sorry, Mr. Chambrun," she said, flushing. "I—"

"You were generously concerned with another human's problem," Chambrun said. "You thought you had a right to make a judgment about telling me .I don't complain. But I have to have those who tell me without making judgments." He turned to John. "There's only one way to fight money if you haven't got it yourself, John. I've had to fight it all my life in this job. It takes a special kind of skill and cynicism. If your father had known the secret a long time ago he might now be the commanding general of NATO. Care to hear it?"

John nodded.

"No matter how rich and powerful a man is, John, he has weaknesses, just like anyone else. So you shadow box him until you find that weakness."

"And then use it against him."

"No, no my dear fellow. That's the secret. Never use it against him—not openly. You keep your knowledge to yourself, a preciously guarded secret, after you have let him know that you know. That's where your father made his mistake, John. He made his secret public; he told the whole world that Aubrey Moon was a coward. If he'd kept it to himself, but let Moon know, afterwards, that he'd seen him push aside that woman and her children—" Chambrun shrugged. "Moon would have given a great deal to have that secret kept. Then, if your father had wanted to be commanding general of NATO, Moon would have promoted the idea, instead of using his money and power to destroy your father.

Your father made the mistake of showing his hole card before the deal was complete."

"You did say cynicism was involved," Alison murmured.

"Of course. So is survival! I don't suppose there is a permanent guest in this hotel about whom I don't know something he wishes I didn't. I make it my business to learn such things. I know the obvious, like which men are cheating on their wives and which wives are cheating on their husbands. I know which ones are spending more than they can afford. In the day-to-day run of things this may not get me much more than a courteous good morning when I might otherwise be ignored. But it has been known to pay off in larger terms." Chambrun chuckled. He chose another fish cake from the chafing dish, wiping his fingers on a paper cocktail napkin. He headed for the door, where he paused. "Any questions, my children?"

"What have you got on Moon?" John asked.

"Moon is a unique case," Chambrun said. "His sins have been public property for a quarter of a century. He has turned them into an asset. He knows the techniques of quiet blackmail as well or better than I do. If he's got anything on you, John, I strongly advise you to take to the woods." He hesitated. "Since I know as much as I do about you, John, it would be interesting to know the rest. But I suppose Lieutenant Hardy has made you promise not to talk."

Chambrun gave John a bland smile, walked out of the office and closed the door behind him.

"There is an astonishing man," Alison said.

TWO

Five minutes later Lieutenant Hardy was in Alison's office, John having called Jerry Dodd in the lobby to ask for the Lieutenant.

Hardy had been a witness to the entire side show in the Grill. He didn't want to listen to what John had to tell him. "What did you see beside the act on stage?" he asked, impatiently.

"I don't get it," John said. "What did I see?"

"Damn it, Wills, you're supposed to be looking for someone who paid you ten grand to kill a man. If we're right about him it's ten to one he was there, watching every moment of Moon's side show. What did you see?"

John shook his head, slowly. "I'm afraid I was like everyone else in the Grill—fascinated with Moon and company. And it became obvious almost at once that he recognized me and passed on something about me to Storm."

"I saw that," Hardy said. "What did you expect? That he'd been pushing you around for twelve years and wouldn't know what you looked like? I saw it, and I saw you; and if I'd paid you money to kill Moon I'd have felt pretty good. If ever I saw a guy who hated another guy, you were it! Right about now Mr. X must think his investment is still in the way of paying off. But you and Miss Barnwell were supposed to be watching for that guy. Didn't either of you see anything?"

"I'm afraid I got so involved personally I forgot what I was there for," John said.

Hardy's smile was sour. "And Miss Barnwell was fighting for her virtue in public. It's a cinch she didn't see anything."

"Thanks, at least, for recognizing my problem," Alison said.

"I learned something about this place in the last twenty-four hours," Hardy said, rubbing his chin with the back of his hand. "Everybody looks alike! Oh, there are fat ones and thin ones, tall ones and short ones, dark ones and light ones—but they all look the same. Dead pan! Superior! Varnish over their hides. But some of those dead pans are cracked down there. They got the same greed for gossip, for dishing the dirt, that anyone else has. But I didn't see the face I was looking for; the face watching you and wondering about you, Wills. I was hoping maybe you saw it. Sometimes, when you're being watched, you can sort of feel it—under your skin."

"I'm sorry," John said. "But there are two other things I have to tell you, which is why I sent for you. Chambrun knows who I am, and he knows I'm up to something for you."

"I thought he was laughing at me when I passed him in the lobby," Hardy said. "He knows everything? The money—the note—what we're doing?"

"We didn't tell him anything," John said. "He told us. He spotted me shortly after I met him. He knew you'd be here talking to us. If he knows anything more than that he didn't say so. But he has ways of finding things out."

"I told you things would leak in this place like a sieve," Hardy said. "Well, let him find out for himself. What we're trying to do is between us—and the Commissioner. What's the other thing?"

John took the crumpled piece of paper Margo Stewart had dropped in his lap in the Grill and handed it to Hardy. "In all the upheaval I forgot to tell you about meeting this girl in the Trapeze Bar last night." He filled the lieutenant and Alison in on the moment with Margo Stewart.

"Moon's secretary," Hardy said. "How do you figure it? What could she want with you?"

"I had the feeling she knows who I am," John said. "It's pretty certain she doesn't love Moon. I'd like to contact her."

"Of course contact her!" Hardy said. "That's what you're here for. Talk to anyone who wants to talk to you. It's our one slim chance of getting a lead to the man we want. Only next time look and listen; don't be had by what's going on around you." The lieutenant shook his head. "You know something? There was only one person I saw in that Grill Room who wasn't reacting the way he felt. Moon let his face slip; he got sore and started to shout. Storm was like a hungry dog, waiting for some crumb of dirt to fall off the table he could print in his column. Miss Barnwell here, angry and embarrassed. You, Wills, burned up at the sight of Moon. The waiters and the Captain, doing their jobs but muttering to each other. The customers, goggle-eyed. Just one person who didn't act what he was feeling."

"Mr. Chambrun," Alison said, in a small voice.

"Right on the nose, Miss Barnwell. He came over to the table to protect you and that banquet manager. He must have been sore at Moon for making a scene. He's said quite openly he hates Moon's guts. He must have had his nose rubbed in plenty the two years Moon has lived here."

"You think Chambrun might be——" John started to ask.

"I just said he was the one person there you couldn't read like a book," Hardy said. He stood up. "See the Stewart girl and let me know what cooks. And stop gaping at the tall buildings. Look and listen to what's going on around you. Keep your eye on the ball. This guy gets a hunch you've quit on him and you're likely to get a good stiff shove from behind."

Making contact with Margo Stewart turned out to be difficult. She lived in the hotel, Alison told John. Moon was something of a night owl. If he wanted to dictate something in the middle of the night he wanted his secretary handy. It had led to gossip that his needs weren't always literary.

"I've never believed it," Alison said. "At least not as an arrangement. In my time here her drinking problem has got worse and worse. I have the feeling she's in one of Moon's specially patented traps. Look, Johnny, I could call the penthouse. Something about publicity for the party—ask her down here."

Mrs. Veach's efficient switchboard had instructions not to put direct calls through to Penthouse M. Jane, the operator, reported presently that Miss Stewart wasn't there. Nor did she answer the phone in her room—804.

Alison had to cover the fashion show that was being held in the Ball Room. John went downstairs with her. In the lobby he talked to Jerry Dodd. The Beaumont's house officer reported having seen Margo Stewart head out the Fifth Avenue entrance about twenty minutes before.

" 'Long about this time of day she usually toddles over to a little grog shop on Madison to lay in the night's supply of liquor. She oughta be back—fifteen or twenty minutes if she plays it as usual."

It was, John thought, a little shocking how much everyone knew about your habits, your hourly movements, in a place like this.

"Come take a look at the pretty girls while you're waiting," Alison suggested. "Jerry'll call you when Miss Stewart gets back."

"Can do," Jerry said.

The Ball Room, which would be the scene of Moon's birthday party on Saturday, had been turned over to a Parisian designer showing a line of next summer's evening clothes. A long runway was set up from the stage at the far end right down to the foyer entrance.

119

Fierce white lights for movie and TV cameras turned the chartreuse walls colorless.

The room was crowded on either side of the runway by people seated at tables, taking notes on each dress as it was shown.

"All professionals," Alison said, over the voice of a man with a strong French accent and a pansy inflection who described each dress on the PA system. John watched the chalk-faced models walking down the long runway, staring blankly yet somehow provocatively, at the male customers. John was reminded of Hardy's comment. These models, like the Beaumont's patrons, all looked alike. Different but all alike.

It didn't seem a likely place for the possible contact he was hoping for. Alison, in terms of her job, had to circulate and speak to people as representative of the hotel. John decided to go back to the lobby and wait for Margo Stewart's return.

Jerry gave him a negative signal, and he appropriated one of the armchairs, covered in a heavy brocade. He could see the corridor to the Fifth Avenue entrance as well as the right angle passage to the one on the side street. Whichever way she returned he'd see Margo Stewart.

He had just lowered his head to light a cigarette when an unfamiliar voice spoke at his elbow.

"Good afternoon, Mr. Wills?"

John looked up. A small, dark man in an expensive black suit, a little too tight in fit, a little too well buttoned up the front, stood smiling at him. The smile was very white, and very fixed. The man's skin was coffee-colored—an East Indian, John thought, or from one of the Arab countries. The man's speech was cultivated, but with a faint accent. He carried a black Malacca walking stick with a heavy silver knob on it.

"My name is Gamayel, Mr. Wills. Ozman Gamayel. I am the bearer of a message."

John felt his pulse accelerate. Perhaps this was it. "I'm listening, Mr. Gamayel," he said.

Gamayel smiled and smiled. "It is a little early in the day for tea, Mr. Wills, but Mrs. Haven thought you might enjoy a drink after your lunchtime experience."

John sighed. That dotty old woman. "I'm sorry," he said. "Thank Mrs. Haven for me. I'm waiting here for someone."

"I think you would find a conversation with Mrs. Haven and me profitable, Mr. MacIver."

John jumped as though he'd been jabbed with a pin. Gamayel had used his father's name without the sightest emphasis, but he made his point with it most effectively.

"You know who I am?" John asked, his eyes hard.

"I know who you are, Mr. Wills—since you prefer to be called Wills. I may even know why you are stopping here at the Beaumont. Shall we go up to see Mrs. Haven?"

John hesitated. "I really am waiting for someone," he said. "Do you object to my leaving word down here where I can be found?"

Amusement crept into Gamayel's bright black eyes. "My dear Mr. Wills, of course leave word. There are three detectives as well as the worthy Mr. Dodd watching you. Would I be so open with my invitation if we intended anything but the most friendly get-together? You see, we are all members of the same club—you, Mrs. Haven, and I."

"Club?"

"The V.A.M. club," Gamayel said. "Victims of Aubrey Moon."

John's face was set in grim lines as he followed Gamayel to the bank of elevators, after telling Jerry Dodd where he was going. The fact that he was Warren MacIver's son was no longer any sort of secret. The minute Moon told Willard Storm it was public property.

But there'd been no time for Storm to relay his scoop to Gamayel.

They rode up the elevator to the roof without further conversation. Gamayel, leaning on his cane, never stopped smiling.

The doorbell of Penthouse L gave off a deep, low chiming note, like a volume-reduced replica of Big Ben. Almost instantly the door was opened by Mrs. Haven herself, wearing an incredible lace-bedecked housecoat that looked like something children had gotten together for a masquerade.

"This is very nice of you, Mrs. Haven," Wills said.

"Come in, Wills," the old woman boomed. "As I told you a while ago, that remains to be seen."

John and Gamayel followed her in. She hadn't waited for them, but had turned and set sail for the interior. John had never seen anything like the room they entered. It looked like a glorified junk shop. There was twice as much furniture as the room could properly hold, most of it Victorian, as far as he could see. Heavy red velvet curtains blotted out the windows. Bookcases overflowed into stacks and piles of volumes on the floor. Sunday papers from the last six months were scattered about. Memory of the Collier brothers flashed into John's mind—except that, he saw at once, there wasn't a speck of dust in the place. What was disorder to him was obviously order to the old woman. If asked for it she could probably put her hand on the editorial page of the *Times* from last June.

An asthmatic growl sounded from behind a whatnot loaded with Staffordshire dogs. Toto's basket was there, and the little spaniel luxuriated on a bright scarlet satin cushion.

"It is too early for tea," Mrs. Haven said, without looking back at them. "Most people who have lived in England for a while like Scotch with tepid water or fizz. What about you, Wills?"

"I've converted to ice," John said. "If there is some—and Scotch—I'd enjoy a spot on the rocks."

Gamayel sat down in an overstuffed armchair, apparently quite at home here. Mrs. Haven moved a large brass cage containing two parakeets and put it on the floor. The cage had been resting on a very modern ice cooler which seemed out of place in the room. With perfect efficiency the old woman made his drink, producing a glass and a bottle from a table hidden behind a carved mahogany love seat. She handed John his Scotch on the rocks.

"This may help you to recover from the shock of seeing my room, Wills—a shock which you are trying very politely to cover. But you have forgotten some of your manners, young man."

"I beg your pardon," John stammered. "I—"

"You haven't spoken to Toto. His feelings will be hurt."

John was sweating, suddenly aware that the room was oppressively hot. She must keep the place at 80 degrees or more. He gave Toto a sickly smile. "Hello, old man," he said.

Toto grunted and turned around on his satin cushion.

"Now," Mrs. Haven said. She gave Gamayel something peach-colored in a delicately tapered liqueur glass. She herself had an Old Fashioned glass, filled to the brim with what looked suspiciously like undiluted bourbon.

"Here is to mutual understanding," Mrs. Haven said. She tossed off half her drink and sat down in a high-backed armchair. Rings glittered on her fingers. She had, John thought, been statuesquely beautiful many years ago. Now she was a grotesque caricature of that past.

"From Ozman's chitchat you have probably gathered I haven't invited you here for entirely social reasons, Wills."

"I gathered it wasn't because of my boyish charm," John said, drily.

"There isn't time for badinage, Wills," she said. "We're all in a hell of a pickle." She tossed off a little more of her drink. Her keen old eyes were aware of John watching her. "My grandmother was a teetotaler," she said. "Wouldn't allow a drop of liquor in the house. Grandfather had to get his at his club. But every night of her life Grandmother drank a water glass of tonic called Prunella. Ninety percent alcohol. She helped to develop in me a contempt for sham. This, in case you are wondering—" and she held up her glass, "is 100 proof Kentucky corn whiskey. It derives its color from the special oak barrels in which it is aged. I'd recommend it to you, Wills, but if you're not used to it it might take the top of your head off. Now, let us get to the agenda for this meeting. Ozman?"

Gamayel looked over the rim of his liqueur glass at John. His white smile was fixed. You couldn't tell whether he was amused, or angry, or just frozen that way.

"We are, of course, a minority of the membership of the club I mentioned, Mr. Wills," he said, his accented voice soft. "But we are on the scene, and I believe it is quite proper for us to act for the whole membership in this emergency."

"Emergency?" John asked.

"Stop playing games with words, Ozman, and get to it," Mrs. Haven said. She turned to John. "There is, of course, no club, no formal membership. But we three, and many others, are all refugees on a cannibal isle. On this occasion the cannibal may have overeaten, but that's not much solace to those of us who are, you might say, in the soup!"

"Do I still have the floor?" Gamayel asked, undisturbed.

"Of course! I told you to go ahead, Ozman."

The fixed, white smile turned John's way. "Mrs. Haven has a way with words herself, Mr. Wills. The cannibal to whom she refers is, of course, Moon. The isle is his world, in which we live, like it or not. You, my dear Wills, have been one of the ingredients in our cannibal's soup pot for twelve years. Moon has been feasting off you, as well as us."

"Ozman!" Mrs. Haven boomed.

"I was merely trying to clarify your simile for Mr. Wills, my dear."

"Well, get to the point!"

"At once. Here is the situation, Mr. Wills. It would seem that some other member of the club, unknown to us I assure you, has rebelled. To pursue Mrs. Haven's simile, you might say that another ingredient in the soup has become highly indigestible."

"Ozman!"

"So sorry, my dear. You drew an amusing picture which I find myself reluctant to abandon. So, without frills, sir. Someone is bent on killing Aubrey, I should guess at his birthday party on Saturday. There would be symbolic overtones in killing him as he celebrates. Should this someone be successful, Mr. Wills, you and I and Mrs. Haven and many others would, you might think, have cause for a celebration of our own. We have all long wished Aubrey dead. But—and there is a big 'but,' Mr. Wills."

The heat, the playing with words, made it difficult for John to concentrate. He wondered if smoking would be considered a fire hazard.

"By all means smoke, Wills," the old woman said, as if she'd read his mind. It wasn't magic. Unconsciously he'd been turning a pack of cigarettes round and round in his damp fingers.

"Time is our problem, Mr. Wills." Gamayel's voice seemed to come from a long way across the room. Its smoothness was hypnotic. "If Aubrey is killed on Saturday night too many of us will be without defenses. Our cannibal will not be through with us, even though he dies of indigestion."

"Ozman!" Old Mrs. Haven pointed a bony finger at John. "Before you are lost in the rigmarole of Ozman's word pictures, Wills, I ask you a direct question. Two questions. Are you here to kill Aubrey Moon? And if you are, are you planning it on your own account, or are you acting as an agent for someone else?"

John struggled to bring the whole thing into focus. He told himself this was what he and Hardy had hoped for. This mad old woman, living in a two hundred thousand dollar junk pile, and her other-world friend were quite capable of being the schemers who had involved him and the Prym girl in this mess. John tried to play it cagey.

"You expect me to admit to comparative strangers that I may be preparing to murder a man?" he asked.

"I expect you to use what little sense God gave you, Wills," the old woman said. Her jeweled fingers fluttered impatiently. "I know all about you, Wills, and your father and what Aubrey has done to both of you. If you have an impulse to put him out of the way I sympathize with it. We also know other things about you. There is no way on earth you could have raised ten thousand dollars to pay to that Prym girl. We also know that, temperamentally, it's not the way you'd go about the job. If you've made up your mind, Wills, you'll do it yourself. We know that. If you are working for yourself I think we can persuade you to abandon the project. If you are, by any chance, an agent for the man who tried the Prym girl first, we hope to persuade you to point him out to us so that he can be made to see that he must drop the idea."

John spoke slowly. "You're saying that you and Mr. Gamayel are trying to protect Moon?"

A deep growl came out of the old woman's throat. "Damn Aubrey!" she said. "To hell with Aubrey. May he die of cancer of the liver and may three black dogs defile his grave!" She was shaking with a kind of fury.

John stared at her, his mouth dropped open.

Gamayel's voice cut across the moment of violent feeling, smooth as syrup. "Simply and directly, Mr. Wills. Aubrey has been prepared for a sudden and violent death for many years. It hasn't happened because most of us have long since been aware that the moment he dies, things that must never come to light will come to light. Aubrey has made certain that none of us will escape punishment."

"A Pandora's box of horrors," Mrs. Haven muttered. The outburst seemed to have exhausted her. Her head rested back against the chair, her dark, painted eyelids closed.

"It is hard for you to believe, Mr. Wills?" Gamayel's voice was frozen behind his smile. "I, for example, have an opportunity to be of service to my country at this moment. I cannot move openly. I dare not. If Moon knew he would take a diabolical pleasure in destroying me. For weeks I have been trying to get him to try to make some sort of bargain, some sort of final deal. He laughs at me, won't even talk to me on the phone. If I am to do what will help my people I must do it secretly—plan to leave here without his knowing. Secret arrangements—and always the fear that he will be too shrewd for me."

"He always is," Mrs. Haven muttered. "Too shrewd for all of us, Wills."

"Our approach to you is direct and without evasion, Mr. Wills, only because there is no time," Gamayel said. "Less than a hundred hours. Should you be planning something on your own—perhaps taking advantage of someone else's scheme—we believe we can show you

127

what a disaster your action would bring to many people as innocent of real wrongdoing as you and your father. If you are acting as an agent for the man who bribed Miss Prym—if, perhaps, you yourself have been bribed—?" He left it as a question.

Here it was again, right on the line. But the pressure was from the wrong direction. They were urging him not to act.

"If I am such an agent—?" he said.

"You must point the way to your principal," Gamayel said, and the smoothness was gone from his voice. This little, dark man was suddenly dangerous. "I sympathize with that principal. He has been driven beyond endurance. But he is acting like a madman. He cares for no one else. He cares nothing for you, Wills, because you will certainly be betrayed once the job is done. The police must have a victim."

"What would you do if you could identify this man?" John asked.

"Persuade him to give up his plan," Mrs. Haven said, "by showing him what will happen to others if he goes through with it."

"And if we cannot persuade him—stop him!" Gamayel said. "By force if necessary. You see, I risk telling you the unvarnished truth, Mr. Wills."

The heat was intolerable. John wiped his face with his handkerchief. "You know so much about me—know it in detail," he said. "Surely you must suspect who this principal is."

"The picture fits no one we know," Mrs. Haven said. "It is someone gone mad, Wills, and we cannot recognize him in his madness."

Was this all the cockeyed truth, John asked himself? Or was it a game to find out just where he stood, how much he would tell, how much he suspected?

"You haven't considered going to the police?" John asked.

"With what?" Gamayel asked. "It is no secret that many people hate Aubrey. He actually enjoys telling the newspapers and the police that there are many people. He has publicly stated that his life insurance consists of having so many enemies who will do almost anything to keep him safe. I can tell the police no more than they already know. But they would ask: 'What does he hold over you? Who are some of the others?'" The corner of Gamayel's mouth twitched. "If I made my story public, Wills, there are people in my country who would dismember me in a dungeon so deep no one would hear me screaming. If I gave other names they might well be publicly disgraced, homes broken, businesses destroyed. There is nothing to be gained by going to the police—unless we can point a finger at the man who is planning to kill Moon!"

"And we don't know where to point," Mrs. Haven said.

John wondered what this strange old woman, so dignified despite her incredible surroundings, could have done to put herself in Moon's power. He half-believed them, but he couldn't run the risk of complete honesty. He lit a fresh cigarette and took a deep drag on it. His shirt was soaking wet from the heat.

"I am aware, as you know, that the police are watching you, Wills," Gamayel said. "Have you talked to them?"

"Let's say they've talked to me," John said. "They know who I am. Moon knows I'm in the hotel. If I wanted to kill him there's not much chance I could get to him."

The old woman put her liquor glass down hard on the table beside her chair. "They'll protect Aubrey as efficiently as they can," she said. "It may not be possible to do him harm and get away with it. Our man has tried through Miss Prym—perhaps through you, Wills

—to get away with it. We can't be sure, that all else failing, he won't do the job and be caught."

"If you hadn't cared about being caught you could have shot Moon to death today at lunch," Gamayel said.

"We have to keep Aubrey alive, God help us!" Mrs. Haven said.

The dark room began to spin in front of John's eyes. He had the powerful impulse to give way to laughter. They were all like crazy children, Moon included, playing parts in a crazily invented melodrama. This was the Beaumont, most expensive and sophisticated hotel in the world; this was New York, the most civilized city. There was no reality to this purple plotting. And yet, only a few months back, the President of the United States, had soberly stated that a moment of madness could turn the whole planet into a flaming funeral pyre. In the face of such a concept, for which science-fiction writers were laughed at ten years ago, could you say that in Moon's world of money, and self-indulgence, and, yes, of cannibalism, the destruction of a few dozen people out of vengeance and spite was impossible?

"I—I wish I could help," John heard himself say. "I can only guess at your difficulties. I sympathize with them. I saw my father with his brains dripping out on the carpet in a cheap hotel room. Moon's done enough harm without being allowed to produce an extra hell after he's dead. I will tell you one solemn truth. Mrs. Haven—and Mr. Gamayel. I don't know who the man is you call the principal. I haven't the remotest idea who he may be. The police are trying to find him and they have no idea where to look."

Mrs. Haven turned her head from side to side. "I don't know why I believe you," she said.

John forced a smile. "I don't know why I believe you," he said.

She waved a dismissing hand at him. "You'd better

go, Wills. Ozman and I will have to revise our thinking."

John caught a glimpse of himself in the elevator mirror as they plummeted toward the lobby with stomach-turning speed. His shirt was stuck to his chest; his blond hair was matted with sweat; his face was red. The elevator man grinned at him.

"I seen other people come out of that sweat box, Mister. You done better than most for the time you was there."

"You wouldn't believe it!" John muttered. "You could cook a roast on the living room table."

He walked out into the lobby, wiping his face with his handkerchief. Jerry Dodd grinned when he saw him.

"I was about to send up one of the boys with an oxygen tank," he said. "I should of warned you. Incidentally, the Stewart girl came in about half an hour ago with her little brown package. I checked with the elevator kid. She went to eight where her own room is."

"Thanks. Where's Hardy?"

"Gone down to headquarters. Said he'd be back around dinner time. You could reach him there now, I guess. Something up?"

"After talking to Mrs. Haven and her pal I don't know whether I'm coming or going," John said. "I'll call him from my room. I need a shower and some dry clothes."

But he didn't go direct to his room. He stopped off at four to see Alison. It was a relief to find her in her office. She gave him an astonished look.

"Don't tell me! You've just finished winning the Boston marathon," she said.

"I've just finished visiting Mrs. Haven."

"Oh, my poor Johnny. And I was the one who told you to be nice to Toto."

"It wasn't a social visit." He gave her a quick resumé of the fantastic conversation. He covered his eyes with his hands when he finished. "It's a funny thing," he said, "I've lost contact with anything ordinary, Alison. I close my eyes and I see figures running for cover on a Korean mountain side—I see them through the sights of my machine gun which I'm firing at them. I see my father with the top of his head blown off. I see Moon—Moon laughing, Moon threatening, Moon with a whip in his hand. I see my mother dying. I see that old woman upstairs, out of another century, and Gamayel. I've seen him in a dozen movies—the smiling, Oriental villain. Yet somehow they're living in terror. I know that. Less than a hundred hours till their world may blow up. I can't see simple things—like the first cup of coffee in the morning. I can't taste that first good cigarette. I can't see walking along the street, looking in shop windows. I can't—"

"Open your eyes!" Alison interrupted, sharply.

Slowly he lowered his hands and stared at her.

"Remember me?" she said. "Nice girl who likes you?"

"It's been twelve years, Alison. Only now the whole thing is spinning faster and faster, with crazier and crazier people on board."

"Johnny!"

"Yes," he said, obediently.

"You go upstairs and have a nice cool shower, and put on a clean shirt, and come back down here. I'll have a nice, iced martini waiting for you. Then we'll go out. We'll eat supper at a hamburger joint. Then we'll go to the Trans-Lux and sit in the balcony, and hold hands, and watch Lana Turner and Efram Zimbalist who've got troubles, too."

"I ought to call Hardy," he said.

"After the martini."

"And would you call the Stewart girl for me? Dodd says she went up to her room a half hour ago."

"I'm beginning to wonder," Alison said, as she picked up the phone and asked for Margo Stewart in 804.

"Wonder what?"

"I would have bet a spring hat I could have had my way with you, Mr. Wills, just by crooking my little finger. I'm losing my touch."

"Alison! I—"

"Johnny dear, let's keep it light. I'm just trying to keep it light." She put down the phone. "Margo doesn't answer. Probably gone up to Penthouse M to check in with the Great Man. I'll keep after her for you while you're changing."

"Would you believe it?" he said. "While I was listening to those two upstairs I found myself thinking about President Kennedy and the end of the world?"

"I think Lana will get Efram in the end." Alison said. "But how'll we ever know for sure if you don't get changed and we don't get started?"

"Okay," he said, laughing in spite of himself. "We'll keep it light!"

He kept it light for about five minutes. It took five minutes to get to the fourteenth floor and down the corridor to the door of his room. He kept it light for another minute while he unlocked the door and fumbled for the switch. He was conscious of something unfamiliar before he got the switch flipped. It was the faint scent of gardenia. He kept it light for another ten seconds while he thought that in a place like the Beaumont it was probably a house rule that the maids should smell sweet.

The switch turned on the lamp on the bedside table and a standing lamp in the corner.

Alison wouldn't be able to get Margo Stewart on the phone. Margo was lying across the foot of his bed, and

133

she wasn't breathing. She wasn't breathing because her head had been smashed in by the Thermos jug that should have been on the bedside table, but was lying on the rug beside the bed, smeared with fresh blood.

PART 4

THE SWEAT WAS COLD on John's body as some instinctive reflex made him back out into the hall and close the door of the room. Then he found that he literally couldn't move. Absurdly he found himself thinking—"To walk you put one foot out in front of you and then step forward with the other." He had just been telling Alison that he couldn't remember anything casual, anything normal. For too long his life had been like crossing a stream on stepping stones, each stone a little island of horror.

The normal thing was to get to the nearest phone and call Jerry Dodd in the lobby. Jerry would know what to do. Then wait for Hardy and Company to ask him what it was all about. He had no answers for them. He could see it stretching out ahead of him. Alibi, Mr. Wills—do you have a real alibi? Do you want us to believe you only met this girl last night? What was she doing in your room? Why did you hit her with the Thermos jug? Was this the pay off, John asked himself, promised by the note writer if he took the money and didn't go through with the job? Was he going to find himself framed for something he hadn't done?

He pushed himself away from the wall so that he had to walk. The momentum took him down the hall to the bank of elevators where he pressed the button. A red

137

light blinked. A car door opened. The elevator operator gave him a startled look. John guessed he must be gray as parchment.

"Lobby, please," a voice said. It was his, strange and unfamiliar. Then as they seemed to drop down in space: "I changed my mind. Four please."

A door opened. A door closed. He walked, noiseless on the thick green carpeting, toward Alison's office— Alison, his only contact with reality.

"Well, that is speed," Alison said. And then she was on her feet, around her desk, her hands holding his shoulders. He must have been waving like an axed tree, he thought. "In God's name, Johnny!"

"Margo Stewart," he said. "In my room. Dead. Killed."

"Johnny!"

"Someone brained her with the Thermos jug."

"What have you done?" Solid, practical Alison.

"I started for Jerry Dodd. I wound up here." He began to laugh. "Turn me around and—and head me in the right direction."

She slapped him hard. "You cut that out, Johnny! Now—sit down there." She gave him a little shove. If the chair hadn't been there, he thought he'd have gone right over on the back of his head.

Alison was on the phone. He couldn't concentrate on the words, but presently she was beside him—kneeling beside him—holding his hands very tightly in hers. Her hands felt hot, but he knew it was really that his hands were like cold marble.

"I've seen a lot of dead people," he said. "In the war. It shouldn't shock me. But—somehow—"

"I never reached her on the phone," Alison said. "She must have gone to your room to wait for you."

To his surprise he said: "Did you ever make that martini?"

"There's a pint of brandy in my desk. You better have some of that."

She brought the bottle. He lifted it to his lips. It was like fire inside him.

Jerry Dodd looked queer without his professional smile.

"You got your key, Mr. Wills?" he asked. "You better come with us." One of Hardy's men was with him.

"Here—the key," John said. "I—I can't go with you, Jerry. I've forgotten how to walk. I—"

"Did you touch anything?"

"No. Yes. The door."

"Nothing inside the room?"

"The—the light switch. I left the lights on. Poor kid."

"Poor kid?"

"Lying there dead—with all the lights on." Unlike the Prym girl, Margo Stewart had obviously had the courage to fight.

"Stay here. Don't go anywhere," Jerry said. "I'll have a guy here in two minutes to watch you—for your own protection. You kill her, Mr. Wills?"

"No—for God's sake!"

"Okay. I just asked."

People came and went. Hardy and Hardy's men, Chambrun, an Assistant District Attorney named Naylor, bald as an egg, and tough. Somebody took John's fingerprints. Somebody brought him a damp cloth to wipe the ink off his fingers. When it began to spin around too fast for him he'd turn his head to look at Alison. She was very pale, but her reassuring smile was there when he asked for it.

Questions, questions, questions—asked and answered mechanically. There were no secrets now. Hardy had been forced to drop the curtain on their little game. Everyone seemed to know that John, like Miss Prym, had taken money to kill Aubrey Moon. There was Naylor's voice from across the room, loud and angry. "None of this cockeyed story can be true. It just can't be true!"

Then Naylor was in front of John, his face zooming in on him like a sudden film close-up. He sat straddling a straight chair, his arms crossed on the back of it, leaning so close to John that the cigar smell on his breath was unpleasant.

"All right, Wills! Let's cut out all this junk about mysterious killers tossing thousands of bucks around. You still say you only met this Stewart girl once?"

"Last night. The Trapeze Bar. She was tight. I—I think she knew who I was."

"Maybe you don't know who you are yourself! Maybe we should ship you down to Bellevue for observation. You never saw her before last night?"

"No."

"But she drops a note in your lap in the Grill Room at lunch time saying she has to see you?"

"Yes."

"Why? Why, Wills? Why?"

"I don't know."

"Come on! Cut it out! Why?"

"I don't know."

"You gave her the key to your room and told her to wait there for you. That's the way it was?"

"No! I never gave her my key. I had my key on me. I let myself into the room with it. I gave it to Jerry Dodd. I—"

"You gave her the key. You took it away from her after you killed her."

"No!"

"What did she want to see you about?"

John leaned back from this hot, angry man. "I don't know."

"She had something on you? Tried to blackmail you? Is that it?"

140

"I keep telling you—I never got to talk to her. I don't know what she wanted."

"You were planning to kill Aubrey Moon. She found out. She had you over a barrel. Is that it?"

"No."

"You weren't planning to kill Moon? You came here, registered under a phony name, were armed with a gun, but you weren't planning to kill Moon?"

"I—I had no plan. Wills is my legal name. I—"

"But you were here to make a plan—scout out the lay of the land. You were making a plan."

"I told Lieutenant Hardy everything."

"Okay, Mr. Wills. You're an innocent schoolgirl. You didn't hate Moon for driving your father to suicide. You didn't hate him for hounding you. You were full of love for him. You were helping Lieutenant Hardy to find a mysterious Mr. X. Then, by the sheerest coincidence, you invite Moon's secretary to your room—and pow! Why? If you were so innocent, so filled with the milk of human kindness?"

"I didn't invite her to my room," John said, slowly, emphasizing each word. "I don't know what she wanted. I didn't kill her. Are my fingerprints on the jug?"

"Are they, Mr. Wills? We don't know the answer to that yet. Maybe you can save us time."

"I never handled it. I never drank out of it."

Naylor pushed his chair back and stood up. "When anybody asks to see me, Mr. Wills, I can usually guess what it's about. He wants to borrow money; he wants lunch. You don't know what she wanted, you say. Well, make a guess."

"Something about Moon, perhaps. If she did know who I was, there might have been something about Moon she wanted to tell me."

"She wanted to help you?"

"Perhaps."

141

"Help you to go through with a killing?" Naylor asked.

"No!"

"Help you with what? She didn't know you, but she wanted to help you, you say."

"You asked me to guess."

Naylor turned away. "I give up," he said. "He's your baby, Hardy. He's either the coolest customer I've seen in a long time, or someone just pinned the tail on the donkey! Get Moon in here."

And now they were close enough to touch—John Wills and Aubrey Moon. The Great Man had evidently been kept waiting in Alison's outer office. His appearance seemed to change the whole feeling in the room. Neither the fuming Naylor nor the stolid Hardy seemed to have the whip hand any longer. Naylor was over-deferential. Hardy looked like a man braced against an attack. Behind Moon, as he came in still wearing the dark suit and Tattersal vest, was Willard Storm.

"Sorry Mr. Storm, this is a police investigation, not a press conference," Naylor said. "You'll have to wait outside."

"Storm stays or I go," the Great Man said, in his thin, sardonic voice. "I'm not swooning with trust for you people, Naylor. You've failed to come up with the man who's threatening me. You've allowed my secretary to be murdered right under your noses. I want someone here with the guts to tell the truth about the general incompetence."

"What goes on here is off the record," Naylor said.

"I will decide what's off the record," Moon said. "And you're wasting time, Mr. Naylor. If I should agree to having Storm excluded it would only mean I'd tell him exactly what happens afterwards." He turned his head and looked directly at John. "What happened, Wills? Weren't her heels round enough to suit you?"

142

It was as if somebody had raised a hand and wiped away the fog in front of John's eyes. The dislocation and confusion of the last hour was swept away. Here was the man who had driven him to the brink of murder—the dye in his hair and mustache were clear at this close range; the cruel eyes in their puffy sockets; the faint scene of cologne. Behind all this was the power of money and fame. If Mrs. Haven was right, dozens of lives depended on his whim. But he was, after all, a man and not a mythical monster. He could and must be fought, and to John's surprise, he felt his own fear melting away.

"You know of a relationship between this man Wills and your secretary, Mr. Moon?" Naylor asked.

John waited quite calmly for the answer. His father had been sworn away by Moon in just such a position.

Moon shrugged. "This man whom you call Wills," he said, "is known to me as John MacIver. Quite frankly, if he was having an affair with Margo behind my back I didn't know of it. But it's in the blood, Naylor. His father was court-martialed from the British Army for romancing his C.O.'s wife in order to get military secrets. The son may well have been romancing my secretary in order to find a way to get at me." He smiled at John, as if he hoped for a violent denial. He looked disappointed when John sat still and silent.

"You don't know that they were having an affair?" Naylor said.

"I don't know that they were." Moon made it sound as though he suspected it.

It was Lieutenant Hardy who turned the direction of Moon's attack. "Mr. Naylor isn't as familiar with this case as I am, Moon," he said. "I've had twenty-four hours to pretty well cover the ground in this plush loony bin. The general consensus of the staff in the hotel is that you were having the affair with Miss Stewart. She lived here. She was on call to you at all

143

hours of the day or night. Let's clear that up. Was she your girl, Moon?"

Moon laughed. "No. Sandy, as I called her, was not my girl. Too scrawny to begin with. Too full of self-pity. And making love to a drunken woman does nothing for the ego. I lean toward the simple nympho, or the talented professional like the late, and I must admit lamented, Miss Prym."

"But you trusted her?" Naylor said. "She was your confidential secretary?"

"I never trusted Sandy with any personal secrets I wasn't quite willing to have broadcast to the general public. You should know, as a lawyer, Naylor, that you can never trust alcoholics or homosexuals."

Naylor pounded on. He seemed quite undisturbed by Moon's destruction of the dead girl's character. "I'm trying to get an answer to a question," he said. "This confidential secretary of yours was trying to make an appointment with Wills. Have you any idea why? You suggest he may have been using her to find a way to get at you. What could she have told him that would help him to do you harm?"

Moon turned to look at John again. "MacIver harm me?"

"He has a motive of sorts," Naylor said.

"He may imagine he has a motive," Moon said, "but one thing I know he hasn't got is the courage to lift a finger against me. For a good ten years now he's been like an East Indian beggar, sitting outside a wailing wall, telling the world how badly he's been treated. Look at him. Here we are, face to face, and he won't rise to any bait. Of course he may be capable of cracking a helpless girl over the head with a water bottle. His father had a slogan he died by. 'Women and children first.' "

John, fighting a tidal wave of anger, felt a hand close hard on his shoulder. He turned his head and looked

144

up at Pierre Chambrun. Chambrun's hooded eyes looked past John at Moon, but his hand was the hand of friendship. It kept John sitting where he was, his jaws clamped together.

"Well, well! The ubiquitous Mr. Chambrun," Moon said, his eyes glittering. "You have a habit of turning up at the most irritating moments, Chambrun."

"The Beaumont is my world, Mr. Moon," Chambrun said, his voice dead level. "Everything that happens in it is my business. I'd like to urge Mr. Naylor to get on with his investigations instead of providing you with a rostrum for your particular brand of filth. I've had enough of it—starting two years back, Moon. I want this thing resolved, and then I want the cleaning women in here to fumigate Miss Barnwell's office."

"I'll handle this my way, Chambrun," Naylor said.

"I'm sure you will. I'll also handle it my way," Chambrun said. "You want facts, I assume. You can't convict anyone without facts. Allowing Moon to have a field day with the characters of the living and the dead isn't going to solve your case. I stood in the doorway there listening to you trying to bully Mr. Wills into admitting he gave his room key to Miss Stewart. Well, I know how she got in the room, and it wasn't with Mr. Wills' key."

"How do you know?" Naylor asked.

"I run a hotel. I know how it works," Chambrun said. "Like you, Naylor, I look for easy answers but I look for them intelligently. Miss Stewart came into the hotel just before four-thirty from the outside. She went up to her floor—eight. She then approached the housekeeper on that floor, a Mrs. Kniffen, and asked to borrow her passkey. She'd left her own key locked in her room, she said. Mrs. Kniffen knew her and trusted her —so she broke a rule because she was on the point of going home for the day. Keys are locked in rooms a dozen times a day. The rule is that the housekeeper

145

goes to the door and lets the tenant in, never parting with her passkey. Mrs. Kniffen was in a hurry. She loaned Miss Stewart her passkey on the promise that Miss Stewart would immediately return it to the night housekeeper who'd presently be taking over. So Miss Stewart took the key—and it hasn't yet been returned."

"The passkey for the eight floor would open rooms on the fourteenth floor?" Hardy asked.

"It would. On any floor."

"We didn't find it in the room or in her purse."

Chambrun shrugged. "The person who killed her may have a use for it." His glance shifted back to Naylor. "You're looking for a simple answer, Counselor, so you brush aside a very complex story that must have a complex answer. Someone did leave ten thousand dollars in the bank for the Prym girl and another ten thousand for Wills. Someone did write notes to them. Someone is plotting to kill Mr. Moon. Don't try to disconnect the Stewart girl's death from those facts. Don't think there's a simple answer, like a backstairs romance between Wills and Miss Stewart. Ever looked at a modern expressionistic painting? It takes time and careful analysis to figure out its real design and purpose. And you and Mr. Moon haven't got much time, Naylor. The painter of this picture has promised us another death by Saturday night."

Naylor stared at the hotel manager, frowning. He was angry, but in spite of that, he was a pro.

"I'm touched by your concern for my safety, Chambrun," Moon said. "We mustn't have any more messes on the rug, must we? Well, I have a little pronouncement of my own, Mr. Naylor. My confidence in you and the police is not earth shaking. I shall use every means in my power to protect myself. This place is crawling with people hostile to me. Have you bothered to talk to that crazy old woman who lives in the penthouse next to mine? She'd twine daisies in her hair if some-

146

thing happened to me. Have you bothered to investigate that phony Egyptian diplomat named Gamayel? He'd buy a box seat to my hanging. As to this man here—John Wills MacIver. You turn him loose again and I warn you I might mistake a nervous nose-blowing for a threat against me. You, Hardy, you've been helpless up to now. Well, I have a license to carry a gun." He patted the pocket of his charcoal gray suit. "I shall use it to protect myself. I serve notice on you now that I'll use it without hesitation and without stopping to ask questions."

"Why don't you move out of here till we get this thing cleared up, Moon?" Naylor asked.

"A man's home is his castle," Moon said. "I choose to make my stand here. Come on, Storm. Let's leave the mice to play."

He went—and they let him go.

TWO

John lifted his hands to cover his face. He felt drained. Keeping himself from answering back had been an exhausting business. He wondered what would have happened if he'd satisfied the urge to take a swing at Moon. The satisfaction would have been worth almost any result.

Hardy came over to stand by John's chair. "I haven't heard the details of your visit upstairs. I just know you were there, talking with Mrs. Haven and Gamayel. What did they want?"

John drew a deep breath. "They wanted help."

"Help? From you?"

It was hard to bring the old woman and Gamayel back into focus.

"Help in doing away with Moon?" Naylor asked.

John shook his head. "Help in protecting him. It's

147

hard to tell you simply. According to them they've been blackmailed by Moon for years—they and many others."

Naylor laughed. "Blackmailed? With his money he's blackmailing people? I'm getting awful sick of you, Wills."

"The trouble with you, Naylor, is that you don't think before you say things," Chambrun said, in that same dead-level voice.

"And I've had about enough from you, Chambrun," Naylor said. "Thanks for the facts, but let us do the investigating."

"Look, Counselor, I know the cats that live in this alley better than anyone," Chambrun said, undisturbed. "They're my business. You put labels on everything— very simple labels. Blackmail to you means getting money out of someone. There are a lot of other things you can get out of people. You can blackmail them into obedience, into slavery. You can blackmail an honest man into becoming a crook. Moon's hobby is playing with human lives; making people do things they don't want to do. It's a kind of power mania. Why not let John finish what he's telling you without labeling him an idiot before he finishes?"

"All right, Wills. Go on with your fairy story," Naylor said, sullenly.

"It sounds a little wild, I admit," John said. "Blackmailing them into keeping him alive, Mr. Naylor. He has something on them. They know if he dies by violence whatever he has on them will be made public. His particular kind of life insurance they called it."

"And how were you supposed to help?" Hardy asked.

"They thought I might have come here to kill him. They even guessed I might have been paid by someone to do the job. They wanted to show me why Moon must go on living. If I'd been paid, they wanted me to tell them by whom. They want to persuade him to drop

148

it. They thought perhaps Hardy had a lead and that I'd tell them what it was. Whatever Moon said about Mrs. Haven and Gamayel, believe me they want him alive and not dead."

"They convinced you of that?" Hardy asked.

"Yes."

"More likely a fishing expedition to find out if we suspected them," Naylor said. "I want to talk to those clucks."

The office door opened and one of Hardy's men came in. Hardy went over to a corner of the room and talked with him for a moment. When he came back he was scowling.

"We've drawn a blank so far," he said. "My men have been checking the elevator men, bellhops, doormen to find out who might have left the fourteenth floor, up or down, in the critical time. No dice."

"If he isn't sitting right there," Naylor said, glaring at John, "he can be miles away by now."

"But he has to come back," Chambrun said, quietly. "His job isn't done. No, Counselor, he's in the hotel—or he will be in the hotel again."

Hardy nodded. "If we buy any of it we have to buy that. I buy it."

"If I were in your shoes, Lieutenant, I'd be asking a lot of questions I haven't heard asked so far."

"For instance?"

Chambrun shrugged. "Mr. Naylor doesn't want me to interfere."

"I'm asking you," Hardy said. "For instance?"

"It's easier for me to accept certain things as facts than it is for you and Naylor, Lieutenant. The business of someone throwing around ten thousand dollar bribes to unlikely people such as the Prym girl and John is more than you can swallow. It becomes an unbelievable charade to you. But in my business I see bigger sums than that thrown down the drain for a whim. You stop believing because you can't swallow the money, no matter how hard you try. I can swallow the money easily enough, but I have trouble with the next step."

"What step?" Hardy was impatient.

"Were the Prym girl and John really expected to kill Moon?" Chambrun asked. "I choke on that because people are my business. Neither one of them has a history of violent behavior. Neither one of them is a killer. They do have one thing in common—a hatred for Moon. But if you were to ask me, a reasonably good judge of people, what they would do when they got the notes and found the money was real I'd say this. I'd say they'd take the money, think about it a while and then reveal the truth. I wouldn't have guessed at suicide, but I'd have guessed Pamela Prym would finally tell someone, just as John told Miss Barnwell."

"So?"

"So my first question would be this, Lieutenant. Were the Prym girl and John expected to kill Moon, or were they expected to reveal the plot against him? Unless the man we're looking for is a fool the answer has to be he wanted them to reveal the plot."

"That doesn't make sense!" Naylor said. "You mean he was just trying to make it tougher for himself?"

"That wouldn't make sense, would it?" Chambrun said. "So my next question would be: Is there really a plot to kill Moon, or is the whole thing a smoke screen to cover some other purpose and plan?"

Hardy whistled softly.

"The murder of the Stewart girl?" Naylor asked.

"We have to consider that, I suppose," Chambrun said. "I'm inclined to reject it. Such elaborate and expensive preparations don't fit what looks like an impromptu and improvised killing. Our man couldn't have known till a half hour before it happened that Miss Stewart was going to get a passkey to John's room. He must have been watching her, following her.

He gets into the room and kills her—with a water bottle! If Miss Stewart was the main target surely he'd have been better prepared. Let's go back and speculate a little further, gentlemen. I answer that second question by saying for the moment I don't believe there is a plot to kill Moon. I think the whole thing is a smoke screen to cover some other purpose and plan. Having answered it that way I say I think the Stewart girl got wind of it somehow, was going to pass it on to John, and got killed for her pains."

"Where does that take you?" Hardy asked.

"So I ask myself question number three," Chambrun said. "I can't guess at the real project, the real plan. But the Stewart girl did. Why didn't she bring what she knows to you, Hardy? Why decide to go to John with it? I can answer that quickly. She was caught in some kind of a Moon trap. She was one of his blackmail victims. He had something on her. It was, we all know, driving her to the nightmare of alcoholics. She chose to go to John because John would sympathize with her problem. He was a Moon victim, too. He might be willing to use her information without destroying her."

"And our friend guessed what she was up to and had to stop her quick," Hardy said.

Chambrun smiled. "You're learning the game fast, Lieutenant."

"What's the next question?"

"All right, question number four: If Miss Stewart chose John because she didn't dare go to the police; if she chose John because his experience with Moon would make him sympathize with her problem then we ask— did what Miss Stewart have to tell John have something to do with Moon? I answer that 'yes.' If it had nothing to do with Moon then she had no reason to be afraid. Which brings us to question number five."

"Go ahead," Hardy said.

Chambrun looked slowly around at his listening audience. John felt the small hairs rising on the back of his neck. He thought he knew where Chambrun was headed.

Chambrun paused to light one of his Egyptian cigarettes. "So, having answered our questions as we have," he said, "we take the plunge. If there is no plot to kill Moon but the whole thing is a smoke screen to cover some other plan; if the Stewart girl was killed because she got wind of it; if she went to John because what she knew was damaging to Moon; then we must ask ourselves if Moon himself is not the man we're looking for?"

"How absurd can you get?" Naylor asked, but he sounded doubtful.

"Does Moon have the money to throw around in the kind of scheme we're supposing?" Chambrun asked. "He does. Does he have the kind of mind that would be intrigued by such elaborate plotting? He does. Who would best know how deeply Miss Prym and John hated Moon and why? Moon himself. Is he a keen enough judge of character to guess how they would act? He is. Do we have any other facts to support our theory? I think we do."

"What other facts?" Hardy asked.

Chambrun took a step across the room to flick a cigarette ash neatly into the tray on Alison's desk. He turned back. "What just happened in this room?"

"What do you mean?"

"I mean the scene played by Moon," Chambrun said. "We are now assuming he is the plotter, the maker of smoke screens. What came out of your conversation with him? He doesn't trust you. He will take steps to protect himself. He has a gun and a license to carry it. He will use it unhesitatingly and without asking questions. So, we are all running around trying to protect him—you Naylor, you Hardy, me, my entire staff. But if we're right, he isn't in danger. If we're right we just finished watching a man use a phony threat against himself to justify a homicide of his own. 'So sorry, gentlemen. I heard a stealthy footstep behind me. I warned you I'd protect myself.' "

"It could be," Hardy muttered.

"He has spent twenty thousand dollars to make certain that no one in the world will suspect that what appears to be a regrettable accident is actually a cold-blooded, premeditated murder. Cheap investment, don't you think, Lieutenant?" Chambrun was smiling, but it was a hard, unamused smile. "I offer you a clincher, gentlemen. When the Prym girl's suicide revealed the plot against him how did Moon behave? Was he frightened to know that there was a plot to assassinate him? He wasn't. You complained he wasn't taking the danger seriously. Yet, what is one of the key things we know about this man? We know he is a physical coward. John Wills' father was driven to suicide because he made that fact public. Moon wasn't frightened by the threat because he knew there was no threat. He knew it was a smoke screen because he'd set it up himself. Now he's made the last preparatory move. He's prepared you in advance for a murder to come. He will commit it quite openly and everyone will feel sorry for him, while Willard Storm lets the world know that it all came about because the police were inefficient in protecting him."

"You believe this theory of yours, don't you?" Naylor asked, the bluster gone out of him.

"I believe it," Chambrun said, "and it scares the hell out of me."

"Why?"

"Because I don't have a glimmer of an answer to the last question we must ask: Who is Moon going to kill?"

Chambrun put out his cigarette. He looked at Hardy, one eyebrow raised in a half amused question. "I can't prove one word of what I'm suggesting," he said. "But I have an instinct for people and their individual gyrations. Moon is an unbelievable character. It's hard to believe the stories about him until you talk to someone like John, who knows the truth about him. I've seen a man like Ozman Gamayel, a man of wealth and importance in his own country, wriggling like a fish on the end of a poison hook. There is only one Moon. Suddenly he seems to have an enemy, just as devious, just as lunatic as he is himself. Moon himself gave me a clue yesterday when he said something about there not being anyone like himself. I got to thinking. There can't be two Moons, I told myself. Then this began to come together and I convinced myself there weren't two Moons; only one Moon, deadly and dangerous."

"There's one flaw in it," Naylor said.

Chambrun's eyes reflected surprise.

"Since an hour after the Prym girl's suicide Moon has been protected," he said. "He may not think it's efficient, but it has been. There have been two men in the hall outside his apartment in round the clock shifts. There have been two men on the roof, also round the clock. Moon left his apartment just twice—today for lunch, and this evening to come down here. Each time he was accompanied by Hardy's men. So he couldn't have gone to the fourteenth floor and killed the Stewart girl. That knocks your theory out unless you assume an accomplice, Chambrun."

Chambrun's smile was almost cheerful. "You had me worried, Counselor. To begin with, of course I don't rule out the possibility of an accomplice. There are hundreds of employees in the hotel. With his money Moon could hire himself a dozen helpers. He could go high enough to buy normally honest people. But I would like to point out to you that Moon could have

154

left his apartment. There is a service entrance—a back stair, a service elevator. You haven't had men there because Moon keeps the service door locked and he was warned not to open it to anyone. Someone could surprise him by coming over the roof gardens. But not the service entrance. You weren't looking for Moon to leave. No one could get to him through the service door without his cooperation, but he can have gone out as often as he wanted without your knowing."

Naylor looked at Hardy. "What d'you think, Hardy?"

"I buy it," Hardy said. "I buy it one hundred per cent. And I don't mind saying it makes me feel like a new man. At least I know what I'm looking for. And the first thing I do is to have that service door watched." He turned and walked quickly out of the office.

"I buy it, too," Naylor said. He walked over to John and held out his hand. "I'm sorry I pushed you around, Mr. Wills. I hope you'll admit my job called for it."

"Sure," John said. He stood up and took Naylor's hand. "I feel as if I was coming up out of a deep well myself." He walked over to Chambrun. "Could I be the person he's after, do you think?"

"Are you dangerous to him?" Chambrun asked. "Not just as an angry man, but as someone who can harm his position, his prestige, his power? I don't think Moon would run this kind of enormous and elaborate risk just because he doesn't like someone."

"He doesn't like anyone but Aubrey Moon," Alison said. "That was a wonderful piece of reasoning, Mr. Chambrun. But what happens now?"

Chambrun shrugged. "I assume Mr. Naylor and Hardy will keep him covered, watching for him to make a move. I assume they may try to check out some things—for example, withdrawal of funds that would match the twenty thousand put in the banks for John and Miss Prym—amounts and the right time. I'd like to see them get samples from the typewriters in Moon's penthouse—match them up against the notes. He can't be charged with anything on my theory. We need some factual evidence. Incidentally, I make one other assumption and it concerns me. He apparently has no intention of leaving the hotel, so I'd say he plans to have his 'unfortunate accident' take place here. From that you have to conclude that his intended victim is somebody who lives in the hotel, or is a member of the staff, or is a constant customer or visitor. I wonder—" He hesitated. "I wonder if Gamayel and Mrs. Haven would be useful if they could see this thing turned upside down—Moon the killer and not the victim?"

THREE

It had been John's first thought that the way to protect Moon's intended victim—because he had no doubt that Chambrun's theory was fact—was to make that theory a matter of public knowledge. It was instantly pointed out to him that the results would all be negative. It would alert Moon, who would abandon his plan and devise another one; Moon would have time to make certain no loose ends, like tracing the money or the typewriter, were picked up; and finally, if any of the news media like newspapers, radio or television were foolish enough to use the story they'd be joined with Chambrun in a whopping slander suit. You couldn't stand in the Beaumont lobby and tap each passerby on the shoulder and say: "In case you're the one, Moon is after you!"

Cat and mouse. Watch the cat and you'll find the mouse hole.

Possible enlightenment from Gamayel and Mrs. Haven was delayed. The old lady had a box at the opera which she occupied every Tuesday evening. She had gone there in her ancient Pierce-Arrow, driven by an equally ancient chauffeur. Gamayel was not with her, but he couldn't be reached in his suite. The doorman on the Fifth Avenue side remembered seeing him walk down the avenue not too long ago. It was Gamayel's custom to take many walks, some short, some long. There was no guessing when he might be back. It was, it seemed, his custom to go to the Blue Lagoon, the hotel's night club, in time for the ten o'clock show. He would then have dinner and see the midnight repeat of the show.

It was Chambrun's suggestion that John and Alison have dinner in the Blue Lagoon.

"You can let me know when Gamayel comes in," he said. "Mrs. Haven won't be back till well after eleven. The Wagnerian cycle plays late."

It was hard to think of things going on quite normally. The need for action was strong in John, but there seemed to be no specific action to take. Moon and Storm were in the penthouse. If Moon made a sudden move to go anywhere, everyone concerned would be instantly alerted. Meanwhile you sat still and waited.

John finally got his shower. The police had moved his belongings into a different room. He dressed in his dinner jacket and waited for Alison in the lobby. She had an apartment, it seemed, just two blocks away from the hotel.

He saw her come through the revolving doors on the side street entrance. As she came toward him, her head held in that proud way, her walk swinging and free, he felt a tightness in his chest. This girl, no matter what the tensions of the moment, was always herself—honest, direct, properly female, unchanged and untouchable.

"You look very pretty," she said to John.

"You, too," he said. She made it easy to laugh at the

ordinary cliché politenesses. She did look pretty, so pretty it hurt.

She took his arm and they walked across the lobby to the entrance of the Blue Lagoon. The captain at the inevitable velvet rope rope led them to a table Chambrun had reserved for them.

The room was dimly lit. An interesting combination of piano, flute, drums and bass played the intricate rhythms of modern jazz.

"Mr. Chambrun has ordered your dinner, Miss Barnwell," the captain said. "The choice of cocktails and wines are yours."

"That martini we never had?" John suggested.

"Fine," Alison said. "Mr. Chambrun is something of a gourmet. I don't think we'll get our hamburger, Johnny."

"We could still hold hands," he said, "even without Lana and Efram."

She gave him a quick, troubled look. "I wonder, Johnny. It's happening awfully fast, isn't it?"

His heart gave a great bang against his ribs. There was no mistaking what she meant. Before he could blurt out what he felt she went on.

"I'm not sure of myself, Johnny. Since I lost the other half of my pound note I've made friends because someone else needed friendship. You needed it and it was easy to give. But—"

"Alison—what?"

"I gave up the idea of anything else. In the middle of this whole monstrous business I find myself aching for it. I—I tell myself it's because I miss Bill so much. Why so much more now after four years? Then I try to remember what he looked like—and he looks like you!"

"Alison!" He reached out for her hand, but she took it away, gently.

"Please, Johnny. When I said we'd hold hands in the

158

movies I thought of it as an ordinary, friendly thing. A nice nothing. But I don't think of it that way now and it's raising hell with me. So could we let it ride until I get to know you? I don't know you, Johnny, except in crisis. You measure up there fine. But what are you like at breakfast, or teaching your wife to play a game or drive a car? What are you like when things are just ordinary and routine?"

"Have you read the papers lately?" he asked quite gravely. "Will we ever live out of crisis in our time? I watched you walk toward me in the lobby and I said to myself—if I could just spend time with her, ordinary, routine time. I think I'd be awfully good at it, Alison—the little of it any of us can hope to have."

The waiter brought the martinis, glasses frosted.

"Let it jell a little, Johnny," she said. "Please?"

"I want to say no, of course. But yes, dear Alison."

She lifted her glass. "To us, Johnny. However it turns out—to us!"

In his office on the fourth floor Pierre Chambrun poured himself a steaming cup of Turkish coffee. His desk was stacked with the day's accumulation of paperwork; orders to be countersigned, reports from the various department heads to be read and approved, business mail which only he could handle, Mr. Amato's detailed plan for the birthday party, a dozen telephone messages ignored throughout the day.

Chambrun left this work untouched. He walked over to the window, coffee cup in hand, and looked out over the blackness of Central Park, punctuated here and there by street lights. A curious anger simmered in this complex little man. The smooth order of his world had been turned upside down by Aubrey Moon. For Chambrun it took on all the aspects of a personal contest. He had been confronted most of his business life by the armor of money. He had developed tech-

159

niques to deal with it: a smooth surface charm, imperturbability, perfect touch with every detail of his operation, a lifelong study of human eccentricities, and a private intelligence service that provided him with information he could use when the heat was on to make things work his way. But this armament was not enough in the contest with Moon. His intelligence service had not provided him with the one important clue he needed. Who was it that Moon was planning to kill? To approach the answer to this you would have to know why Moon had gone to such elaborate pains to set up his killing.

What could harm Moon, he asked himself? The Great Man's life must be full of stories as unpleasant as the MacIver tale. He would laugh at anyone who threatened to reveal his cruelties. His reputation had been built on a legend of sadism. Could he have committed a crime that someone was now ready to expose? If so, why was the someone waiting to make his revelation? He couldn't be touched financially.

The answer, Chambrun told himself, must lie somewhere in this man's warped personality. What was his greatest weakness? Vanity. Inordinate vanity. A hunger for the spotlight. It didn't matter if what the spotlight revealed was evil, as long as he stayed downstage, front, larger than life. He had spent a dozen years persecuting the MacIver family because his vanity had been hurt by Warren MacIver's public exposure of his cowardice. A relatively small puncture in the area of his vanity could turn Moon into a relentless enemy.

Chambrun walked back to his desk and put down his empty coffee cup. His smile was wry. The "why" could be so absurd that you'd never guess it. Margo Stewart could well have been killed because she was about to reveal that the Great Man had no hair on his chest. More seriously, that he was impotent and all his talk of female conquests was a fraud. That kind of thing

160

could turn Moon's normal sadism into a homicidal frenzy. But where to look for it? The Stewart girl couldn't have known the real story or her death wouldn't have come about so haphazardly. Something she knew would certainly have put them on trial, but she had not been the main target. Her killing would have been better planned in that case.

Chambrun sat down at his desk and pushed aside the accumulation of paperwork. He picked up the morning newspapers and began a second reading of everything that had been printed about Moon. Somewhere there had to be a clue, a lead, a signpost. He reached for his phone and asked to be connected with Penthouse M. The phone was busy.

"Been busy for some time, Mr. Chambrun. Mr. Storm is dictating tomorrow's column to his syndicate."

"Get me Mr. Amato."

"I think he's gone home, sir."

Chambrun put down the phone with a little grimace of impatience. He wanted to get hold of the guest list for the birthday party. He had the feeling the name of the intended victim would be on that list. Moon would have it there, even though he knew that person wouldn't attend. To leave it off would be to draw attention to the omission. Amato undoubtedly had the list, because place cards were to be hand painted.

Chambrun started to get up from his chair when something in the *Tribune* caught his eye. He stood looking down at it for a long time and then he began, unconsciously, to whistle softly. Finally he picked up the phone again.

"Get me Mr. Amato at his home," he said.

Lieutenant Hardy may not have had the quicksilver sharpness of a fictional detective, but he was thorough and dogged. He had, as he said at the time, "bought"

Chambrun's theory about Moon without reservation. He was fully aware of the problems it presented.

They couldn't touch Moon—not yet. His first thought had been to arrest him and put him in protective custody. On the basis of the supposed threat against Moon's life the police would be justified in protecting him. He also knew that Moon's lawyer would have him out on a habeas writ before they could hope to get enough on him to hold him on a real charge.

The first thing to do was to go through the motions of complete protection here at the Beaumont. Meanwhile there were two small leads to follow—the bank and the typewriters. A detective named Gruber was sent to the penthouse to get the typewriter samples. If Moon made a stink about it, Gruber was to tell him they were checking out the machines against some papers found in the Stewart girl's belongings. Let Moon sweat over that a little.

Hardy got on the phone, trying to locate officials at Moon's bank and the Waltham Trust. He hoped to find someone to go to each of the banks with him and go through the records. If withdrawals from Moon's account matched the time of the deposits in the Waltham Trust, they'd have something. It wouldn't hang Moon. Large withdrawals wouldn't be an oddity for a man who gave forty thousand dollar dinner parties. They might never link the two things, but it would be enough to prove to Hardy that they were on the right track. Later they might make the coincidence look fishy.

Hardy was hit by a minor frustration in his efforts. There was no way to look at records until the next morning. The right men couldn't be found. Records were kept in vaults governed by time locks that wouldn't open until then.

He had just finished his phoning when Detective Gruber reported. There was only one typewriter in Moon's apartment.

"He dictates everything he writes to a tape recorder," Gruber said. "Then the Stewart girl typed it up for him. I got samples from the machine—an Underwood. They don't match."

Hardy scowled down at the notes.

"It doesn't mean anything though," Gruber said, cheerfully. "The machine's rented. This one replaced an older one about a month ago. That'd be four or five weeks after the notes to Prym and Wills were written. By this time the company has probably refurbished the original machine so that its characteristics would be changed."

"Damn," Hardy said. "How did Moon take it?"

"I didn't see him," Gruber said. "Willard Storm was there. Moon was resting. Storm made a big thing about what an exhausting day it had been for the Great Man. Storm had no objections to my taking samples from the machine."

"No wonder you look so cheerful," Hardy said. "Moon would have given you a real rough time—just for the fun of it."

Blocked in both directions, Hardy suddenly felt uneasy. He wanted to see for himself that everything was exactly as he'd ordered it to be. He took an elevator up to the penthouse floor. Two of his men, supplied with chairs by the housekeeper, were stationed outside the door of Penthouse M. They reported Moon had had no visitors except Gruber, and Storm who was still inside with him, since he'd returned from the questioning downstairs a couple of hours ago.

Hardy went out the fire exit onto the roof. The two men there were huddled together. The February night was bitter cold.

"We're gonna freeze to death out here, Lieutenant," one of them said. "Couldn't we take it in shifts?"

"I want two men out here," Hardy said. "I'll get two other men to spell you."

"How about some coffee?"

"I'll send some up to you," Hardy said. He glanced at the dark windows of the adjoining penthouse. Mrs. Haven, he remembered, was at the opera. "Just bear in mind what I told you," he said. "Someone may try to get into Moon's place, but what I'm really looking for is Moon trying to get out!"

He went back inside, rubbing his hands. To check with his man on the service stairs, placed there after Chambrun's exposition, he either had to go through Moon's apartment or down a flight and into the service stairs from there. He didn't want an encounter with Moon just then so he walked down, went along the corridor and started up the service stairs from there.

He'd only climbed a few steps when he saw his man sprawled head downward on the stairs.

A cold rage swept over Hardy. The man had been slugged from behind. There was an ugly bruise and cut at the nape of his neck. His breathing was uneven; a badly hurt man. Hardy moved him so that he lay in more level position. Then he ran up the last steps to the door of Moon's apartment. He rang the bell, trying the locked door at the same time. He kept a finger on the bell and pounded on the door with his other hand.

It seemed an endless time before he heard the inside bolt being slid back, a chain rattle, and the door opened inward. Willard Storm, eyes angry behind his glasses, stood there.

"What the hell's the matter with you?" he demanded. "Can't you come to the front door like a human being?"

Hardy pushed past him into the kitchen. "Where's Moon?"

"He's asleep—or he was asleep until you started breaking down the walls."

"Get on the phone and call the house doctor," Hardy said. "My man out here's been hurt."

"Wait a minute!" Storm said. "You can't disturb Mr. Moon. I—"

"Get on that phone!" Hardy shouted.

He knew, before he had gone ten steps into the incense-loaded apartment, that he wasn't going to find Moon.

FOUR

There were no current signs of Moon anywhere in the penthouse. The beds in his room and the guest room were as the maid had left them that morning.

Hardy went to the front door and summoned the two men outside. Storm, his eyes bright with excitement, had called the house doctor. The two detectives carried the injured man up into the apartment while Hardy got Jerry Dodd on the phone.

"Moon's loose," he said. "Get every street exit covered, Jerry. Use my men, your men, everyone you can trust. If he gives you any trouble let him have one for me. One of my boys may have a fractured skull. Where's Chambrun?"

"You make it sound as though you were after Mr. Moon," Storm said. "Obviously the killer you're supposed to be looking for slugged your man, got in here with a passkey, and took Mr. Moon away."

Hardy, who had asked the operator to connect him with Chambrun, faced the columnist, his eyes cold as two newly minted dimes. "Just keep still, Storm. You can be damned certain you'll have plenty of time to talk in a minute or two."

Chambrun's voice came over the wire.

"Moon's gone," Hardy told him. "Went out the service entrance, slugged my man, and got away."

"He must know we're on to him," Chambrun said.

165

"I've told Jerry to seal up the place, but can he cover it all? How about the service entrance itself, kitchens, what have you?"

"Let's not take time to talk about it," Chambrun said. "If he's still in the hotel five minutes from now he'll stay in it."

Hardy put down the phone and turned to Storm. "You wanted to talk, Storm. Well, now's your chance."

"Don't shove me around, Hardy," Storm said. "You fumbled this from the beginning and you fumbled it again."

Hardy put his hand against Storm's chest and gave a shove. Storm sat down hard in an overstuffed armchair. The eyes behind his black-rimmed glasses were suddenly frightened.

"It's not the healthiest thing in the world for you to start pushing the press around, Hardy. If anything's happened to Moon you're going to need us on your side, boy. You're going to need us bad!"

"Take a deep breath, Storm, and listen to me." Hardy turned to one of the detectives who appeared in the doorway. "Bring those guys in off the roof. They're needed inside. How's Palmer?"

"He's hurt bad, Lieutenant."

"Doctor's on his way up. One of you stay here with me. The rest of you report to Chambrun in his office on the fourth floor. He'll know where to send you. I want Moon and I want him quick."

"Right, Lieutenant."

Hardy turned back to Storm. "Okay, buster," he said. "You got no audience but me, so let's have it straight—without any fancy talk or threats. I got nothing to lose but my job, and if I have to knock in your pretty teeth to make you come clean. I will. You and Moon came up here after we talked to you in the PR office earlier. What happened after you got in here?"

166

"I don't have to take this kind of bullying from you, Lieutenant. I—"

Hardy took a threatening step toward him. "You'll have to take it, buster, whatever your drag is afterwards. I want answers and I want 'em fast. What happened after you and Moon got here?"

Storm must have seen there wasn't an ounce of bluff in Hardy. He moistened his lips. "Nothing happened," he said. "We came in. Moon poured me a drink. I had to get my column out and asked him if I could phone it in from here. He said I could. He was pooped. He wanted to lie down for a while. It's hard to remember the guy's seventy-five. A day like this took it out of him."

"Get on with it," Hardy said. "I'll cry for him some other time."

Storm spread his hands. "That's all there is. I sat down at the desk over there to make some notes. He went back down the hall to his room. I'd been working half an hour or so when your man came in here to check the typewriter. What the hell was that all about?"

"He was following orders. So you were working at the desk."

"A little while after your guy left I called my office and dictated my column. I'd just hung up the phone when you started to bang on the back door. I naturally assumed Aubrey was still in his room. I hurried out to the kitchen to let you in so you wouldn't wake him."

"So you worked here all by yourself, making notes, except for the time Gruber was here? After that a long phone call. Right?"

"Right."

"And you say you think it's obvious someone slugged my man, opened the back door with a passkey, and spirited brother Moon out of here?"

"What else?"

"Without your hearing anything?"

"I closed the door to the hall so my talking on the phone wouldn't disturb him. I didn't hear anything so that's the way it must have been."

Hardy boiled over. "You stupid fool," he said. "When you let me in the back door you had to slide open a bolt and take off a safety chain before you let me in. I suppose the guy who silently carried Moon out of the apartment was able to slide that bolt and hook the chain from the other side of the door after he went out? Don't look at me like a dummy! You were the only one in the apartment. You closed and locked that door after Moon went out. Who else?"

Storm's face looked like a white cheese.

"An accessory to a murder goes to the electric chair right along with the guy who does the killing, buster. You got a slim chance of saving your own neck by telling me exactly what happened here. It's a slim chance, because if Moon gets to do what I think he's going to do all the talking in the world will come too late to do you any good."

A little rivulet of sweat ran down Storm's cheek. "I don't know what you're talking about," he said. "You keep making it sound as though Moon was going to kill someone. He's the one in danger, for God's sake! So I did let him out the back door, right after we got here. He said he was sick of being followed around by by you and your cops. He said there was someone he wanted to see without the whole world knowing about it. The way he said it—the way he smiled—I figure it's a dame. The old boy probably has a tootsie stashed away in the hotel somewhere. Somebody'll know about it. You can't keep that kind of thing a secret. You'll find him there."

"You were to let him in when he came back?"

"No. He'd come back the regular way, he said, and

168

give your men a surprise. He'd show you up for the fathead you are, he said, for not having the service stairs covered." Storm raised a defensive hand. "I'm just quoting what he said."

Hardy drew a deep breath. It could be true. It was a good half hour after Moon returned to his penthouse from Alison's office before he'd posted a man on the service stairs—the time it took for Chambrun to develop his theory. Storm could be quite innocent of anything except trying to play a game on the police. So what had happened to that notion? Why had Moon changed his mind and returned by the service stairs? Why had he slugged Palmer? All he had to do was laugh at Palmer and ask to be let in.

Then the answer came to Hardy. If Palmer hadn't seen who hit him, Moon would be in the position of claiming that this proved how close the mythical killer had been to reaching him—just a few steps from his back door.

The front doorbell rang and Hardy's man crossed the room in a hurry to let in the doctor.

"Stay with him," Hardy ordered his man, pointing at Storm. "Don't let him out of that chair. Don't let him near a phone."

"Am I under arrest?" Storm asked. Some of his self-confidence was returning.

"You're damn right," Hardy said. "Homicide, before the fact."

"I've a right to get in touch with my lawyer," Storm said.

"You can try," Hardy said. "If he tries, Joe, take him apart."

"I'll break you for this, Hardy," Storm said.

"Could be. And if I think you got a chance, buster, I may break you first—slowly and into small pieces." He followed the doctor into the bedroom where the injured Palmer lay.

The second course of their dinner, a delicate green turtle soup, was just being served when John and Alison saw Jerry Dodd bearing down on them from the entrance to the Blue Lagoon. His professional cheerfulness was notably missing.

"Sorry," he said. "You two are wanted in Chambrun's office."

"Oh Jerry!" Alison said. "We've only just started dinner. Maybe half an hour?"

"Moon's loose," Jerry said. "Slugged one of Hardy's men. Anyone he might have an eye on's wanted in Chambrun's office. That's you, Mr. Wills. The boss wants Miss Barnwell, too. He thinks Moon might be interested in her."

"In me?" Alison said, her eyes wide.

"He's blown his lid," Jerry said. "The boss thinks you might be used to put some kind of pressure on Mr. Wills. Sorry about the soup."

They followed Jerry across the lobby to the bank of elevators. Anyone familiar with the hotel routines would have been conscious of unusual tensions. There were cops at the revolving doors; plain-clothes men were hurrying from one bar and restaurant room to another. Just as they reached the elevators Mr. Amato came bustling toward them from the outside. Somehow he looked absurd in a gaudy plaid sports jacket, tweed top coat and an Alpine hat. The black coat and striped trousers were his working uniform and he hadn't stopped to change into them. He carried a manila envelope under his arm.

"Is the party off?" he asked eagerly. "Mr. Chambrun asked me to rush down here with the guest list. I took it home so I could drop it off with the artist who paints the place cards in the morning. Is it off?"

"My guess is you can comfort your ulcer," Jerry said.

They shot up to four and along the corridor into

170

Chambrun's office. John was suddenly aware that Alison's hand was locked tightly in his.

The office was crowded. John saw that Willard Storm, looking a lot less like a Madison Avenue smoothie, was huddled in a chair in a corner. Chambrun was behind his desk, bending over a set of blueprints. Hardy and half a dozen plain-clothes men were bunched around him.

Hardy pointed at the prints. "It's hard to see how he could have gotten out of the hotel without being seen," he said. "You say there's a watchman on the service entrances at night?"

"After delivery hours," Chambrun said. "As a matter of fact you can't deliver an ice cube to this place without being checked. The trouble is no one would have a reason to stop Moon until fifteen minutes ago. It might seem odd for him to leave the hotel by way of the kitchens, but he's an odd guy."

"But he'd be remembered! He's known!" Hardy said.

Chambrun's lips were tight. "He hasn't been remembered so far," he said. "But it takes time to check, Lieutenant. There are over twelve hundred employees on duty at this moment."

"Well, there's no place he could go but down," Hardy said. He began giving orders to his men, pointing to certain check points on the blueprints.

The motherly Mrs. Veach, chief telephone operator, appeared at that moment carrying a telephone with a jack attachment and a head set. Chambrun smiled at her.

"Thanks for your ever-cooperative spirit, Mrs. Veach. Set yourself up over there at that big table." He carried the blueprints over to her. "Calls will be coming in from all over the hotel in a few minutes. They'll tell you that a certain exit is covered. Mark it on the print. The housekeepers on each floor are searching broom closets, linen rooms, and checking each room and

171

apartment on every floor. When you are given the all clear, mark that floor off."

"If you had some thumbtacks, Mr. Chambrun, it would show up faster on these blueprints."

"Good girl," Chambrun said. He produced thumbtacks from his desk. Mrs. Veach plugged her phone into a jack in the wall board. There was an instant buzzing. Mrs. Veach took the call and promptly placed a thumbtack in the blueprint. Chambrun glanced at it, gave her a fatherly pat on the shoulder and turned away to confront the panting Amato.

"Thanks for being so quick, Amato," he said.

"Is the party off, Mr. Chambrun? What's going on? Has he called off the party?"

Chambrun smiled at him. "The party's off, my friend. Go home and get yourself drunk. It'll do your ulcer more good than you imagine. Just leave me that list."

Amato handed over the list. "I prayed," he said. "I prayed all the way down in the taxi. I didn't really believe, but I prayed." He went out, almost dancing, without ever having found out what was going on.

The office was quiet now except for the almost constant buzzing of Mrs. Veach's phone. The blueprints were rapidly accumulating tacks. Hardy watched over her shoulder, sucking on his lower lip, doing a little praying himself. He was waiting for a call that wouldn't result in a thumbtack. That would mean someone had seen Moon.

Chambrun spoke to Jerry Dodd. "Our two friends?"

"Gamayel hasn't shown," Jerry said, "but the men at both entrances are ready to flag him when he comes in. I sent Jack Stroehmeyer to the Opera House. He'll bring Mrs. Haven back—ride with her every step of the way."

"I guess that's all we can do," Chambrun said. He gave John and Alison a tight, tired little smile. "Sorry about the dinner, children. Jerry brought you up to date?"

"We don't really know what's happened," Alison said.

Chambrun gave it to them. "Slugging the man Palmer doesn't make too much sense, unless Moon's run completely amok. I felt we couldn't take the chance that he hasn't. He might take a swipe at anyone he has reason to dislike."

"He must have got out of the hotel," John said. "Surely he couldn't stay hidden for five minutes here. Everybody knows him."

Chambrun waved wearily toward Mrs. Veach's blueprints. "Have you the remotest idea how many places there are to hide in a place like this? Excuse me a minute. I want to look at this list." He unfolded the papers Amato had brought him. He was obviously looking for a specific name, and he found it almost at once. His mouth tightened. He turned to Jerry.

"Was Stroehmeyer going to phone you from the Opera House, Jerry?"

"Well, no, Mr. Chambrun. That is unless something went wrong—she wasn't there or something?"

"Well that's that. I want you downstairs, Jerry. The minute her car gets here I want her covered. No one's to get anywhere near her from the car to this office except you and Stroehmeyer. Understand?"

"Can do," Jerry said, and took off.

"Mrs. Haven and Gamayel are our only possible keys to this puzzle," Chambrun explained to John and Alison. "It's something of a disaster they're both out of the hotel." He turned to look at Mrs. Veach. The phone had buzzed and she was putting another thumbtack in the blueprint.

"What can I do to help?" John asked.

"Sit tight," Chambrun said. "When Mrs. Haven gets here you and Alison may both be useful."

"You think she may have the answer for you?"

The heavy lids of Chambrun's eyes were almost closed. "I think she is the answer," he said.

At just a little after ten o'clock the ancient Pierce-Arrow pulled up at the side entrance to the Beaumont. The old man driving the car got out and walked around to open the door. Inside the car Mrs. George Haven sat rigidly upright, making no move. Gently, almost reverentially, the old chauffeur removed a fur robe from her knees. Jack Stroehmeyer, Jerry Dodd's man, who had been sitting beside Mrs. Haven in embarrassed silence, got out the far side of the car and came around to the sidewalk. From inside the hotel Jerry Dodd and two policemen appeared.

The old chauffeur offered his hand and Mrs. Haven got slowly out of the car.

"Sorry we had to break up your evening, Mrs. Haven," Jerry said.

"I sincerely hope for your sake, Dodd, your employer has a reasonable explanation for this interference with my evening. Do you realize Nilsson was singing tonight?" She brushed away Jerry's arm. "I don't need your help, Dodd. Otto is used to my ways."

The old chauffeur, who scarcely came up to Mrs. Haven's shoulder, took her arm and helped her across the pavement to the revolving door.

"Good night, Otto."

"Good night, Madam."

Mrs. Haven propelled herself violently through the door and set sail for the far end of the lobby. Dodd and Stroehmeyer had literally to run to catch up with her. Her blue evening coat, lined with white fox, trailed out behind her. The dress under it was out of *Great Expectations*. At the elevator she spun on Jerry.

"I can get to my rooms without your help, Dodd."

"I'm afraid we have to go to Mr. Chambrun's office, ma'am."

"If Chambrun wants to explain this extraordinary evening he can come to me," Mrs. Haven said. "Mind you, Dodd, I've never trusted the man. In the seven months I've lived here he's never once spoken to Toto. Beware a man who doesn't like dogs, Dodd."

"It's a police matter, Mrs. Haven," Jerry said. "I'm afraid you'll have to go to Mr. Chambrun's office."

"Police matter!" Her voice boomed out so that people at the far end of the lobby turned.

"Something to do with Mr. Moon, ma'am. Please, this way."

Her hand, like a bony claw covered with rings, closed over his wrist. "The plot against Mr. Moon has been successful?" she asked.

"No, ma'am. At least we think not. Lieutenant Hardy and Mr. Chambrun will tell you what it's all about, ma'am."

She leaned on him so hard he thought she was suddenly ill. But after a moment she straightened up and walked into the waiting elevator. They rode to four in silence. Stroehmeyer got out first and looked up and down the corridor. Mrs. Haven followed him. Jerry opened the office door for her, and she sailed in, evidently recovered from her moment of weakness.

The first person she spotted as she made her entrance was John Wills. There was an angry glitter in her eyes. "Do I have you to thank for this, Wills?"

"I'm sorry, Mrs. Haven," John said. "I have told Lieutenant Hardy and Mr. Chambrun—and Alison—about our visit. But that isn't why they've asked you to come here."

"Asked me! I was literally dragged out of my opera box by that young man—and Nilsson in her second act! So you were unwilling for any of us to have any

175

privacy, Wills. I am disappointed. Not in you, but in my own judgment of you."

"So much has happened since I saw you, Mrs. Haven. You didn't know that Moon's secretary had been murdered?"

"I think," Chambrun said, gently, "it would be better if Mrs. Haven sat down." He bowed toward the comfortable green leather armchair by his desk.

"Your headwaiter's manners will get you nowhere with me, Chambrun. A man who could ignore an innocent little dog for seven months—" But she draped herself in the armchair.

Hardy still stood by Mrs. Veach's table, an expression of awe on his face.

"Would you care for some coffee, Mrs. Haven?" Chambrun asked.

"I would not! If you have some good bonded bourbon whiskey—?"

"At once."

While Chambrun went to the cabinet behind his desk Alison knelt beside the old woman's chair. "What's happened is pretty shocking, Mrs. Haven," she said. "It seems there is no plot to kill Mr. Moon."

"No plot!"

"No plot against Moon. He is the plotter and the plot is against one of you."

"What do you mean, Barnwell, by 'one of you'?"

"The club," John said. "Mr. Gamayel's club."

Chambrun came back with a two-ounce whiskey glass of bourbon and handed it to the old woman.

"You call that a drink?" She tossed it off in one large gulp. "Will somebody make some sense out of this for me. I should like to know what you think justifies tearing me forcibly away from a performance of *Seigfried*."

In a quiet, almost conversational tone, Chambrun

brought the old woman up to date. She listened, sitting very straight in her chair.

"So you see, Mrs. Haven," Chambrun concluded, "the man is aiming at someone and we haven't the slightest notion who it may be. Mr. Wills led us to believe that you and Mr. Gamayel might be able to help. We haven't been able to locate Mr. Gamayel. We had to bring you here in the hope of saving a life. I think even the great Nilsson would forgive you if she knew why you'd walked out on her."

"Don't be an idiot, Chambrun," the old woman said, in a hard unfamiliar voice. She looked straight past and through them as though they weren't there.

"Let me be very precise, Mrs. Haven," Chambrun said. "It wasn't just to get information from you that we brought you here. It seemed quite possible to me that you, yourself, were the target."

"What nonsense," she said. But she didn't look at him.

He turned and picked up that morning's copy of the photographs—Moon with G.B.S., Moon with the Italian film star, Moon with the Prince of Wales, and the studio portrait of the vanished Viola Brooke. He handed it to Mrs. Haven. She looked at it and glanced up at him, sharply.

"I don't mean to wound you, Mrs. Haven, by telling you that I was only twelve years old at the time it happened—1922, wasn't it? I don't think I had ever seen a picture of Viola Brooke until today. It didn't click with me until I looked at it again tonight."

"Viola Brooke is dead," the old woman said, her voice harsh.

"I'm sure all of us in this room would like to respect your wishes, Mrs. Haven. But bear in mind Aubrey Moon knows she is not dead. I think he is mortally afraid of her, Mrs. Haven. I think he means to kill her. You could tell us why and you could help us protect her."

The old woman was silent for a long time in a room in which nobody else seemed to be breathing.

"You're right, of course," she said, in a voice so low they could scarcely hear her. "I am Viola Brooke."

FIVE

John Wills found himself staring at the old woman with a kind of shocked fascination. This was the famous beauty who, forty years ago, had disappeared from her dressing room at a West End theatre in the middle of a performance and never had been heard of again! For almost a year the newspapers had kept her story alive, and had finally given up when there'd been no clues at all to her fate. Viola Brooke who, from all accounts, had almost certainly been Moon's mistress for a number of years after the first World War!

The old woman's eyes turned to Willard Storm, huddled in a chair across the office. He was leaning forward, his eyes bright behind the black-rimmed glasses. Here was a story!

"I tell you the truth, Chambrun," the old woman said, "at great cost to myself. That worm—" and she pointed a bony finger at Storm, "—that worm will have a field day with me. Must he be present if I am to go on?"

"Don't worry about him, Mrs. Haven," Hardy said. "He'll cooperate. He has to, if he doesn't want the book thrown at him."

"At the age of seventy-three a woman still has her vanity," Mrs. Haven said to no one in particular. "Some women retain their beauty in old age. For many reasons I have had to play another game. I have made myself comic to avoid recognition. For thirty-five of those

years it was a joyful game. The last five years have
been a kind of hell."

"Your husband died five years ago, Mrs. Haven?"
Chambrun asked, gently.

She nodded, her heavily painted eyelids closed.

"It's not our wish to make things painful for you,
Mrs. Haven," Chambrun said. "In terms of our problem
there are certain things we need to know. Ozman
Gamayel is your friend?"

"A good, loyal friend."

"Does he know the truth about you, Mrs. Haven?"

"He does. He and my chauffeur, Otto—and Aubrey
—are the only people who did know until now."

"Have you any idea where Mr. Gamayel is?"

"No. He left my apartment when it was time for me
to dress for the opera."

"You neither of you knew then about Miss Stewart's
murder?"

"I didn't know until you told me just now. Ozman
didn't know when he left me."

"How much of the story you told John Wills is
true?"

"Story?" The old woman looked at John. "I had
supposed Wills accepted it as fact. It is quite true there
are a score or more people who will be publicly and
privately destroyed if Aubrey Moon dies a violent death.
He has collected evidence against these people and if
he should die violently, that evidence will be made
public, perhaps by his lawyer or someone he has named
trustee of his affairs. Ozman and I felt it was vital to
try to keep him alive. We thought Wills, who had been
victimized by Aubrey, would understand—might be
able to help."

"Moon's violent death could do you great harm,
Mrs. Haven?"

Her mountainous bosom rose and fell in a long sigh.
"I least of any," she said. "My privacy destroyed, yes.

My true identity made public with all the accompanying hurrah, yes. The others would face real disaster."

"But you allied yourself with them even though the personal danger to you wasn't great as theirs?"

"I did, Chambrun. I did, because if it hadn't been for me these people—and many others like Wills' father and Wills himself—would not have had a lifetime of hell provided by Aubrey. I am to blame, because I was selfish." She looked straight at John. "I am to blame for your father's death, Wills, because I was only concerned with myself."

"I find that hard to believe, Mrs. Haven," Chambrun said.

"It's true," she said, "though I must say in my own defense that for thirty-five years I had no idea what was going on; what Aubrey was doing with his life and to other lives. You might as well know it all, Chambrun." Her bony hands were locked together in her lap.

Chambrun picked up the empty shot glass and went over to the sideboard. He came back a moment later with an Old Fashioned glass filled to the brim. The old woman gave him a bright smile. That smile must have been devastatingly charming forty years ago.

"That," she said, "is more like it." She drank almost half the glass and put it down on the desk. "I lived with Aubrey Moon for five years, Chambrun. And when I say it I feel as though I might be saying, 'I had leprosy for five years.' I feel that way now, but in the beginning it was something else. The last year of the war—the first war. Everything wild and gay and life lived for the moment. Aubrey was charming in those days. It was before fame had touched him, but of course even then he was fabulously rich. Anything we wanted to do we did; anything we wanted to have we had. I was at the top of the ladder in my own profession. I didn't realize it at the time, but possessing me added to Aubrey's prestige. He was rich, and people thought he must be quite a man to have acquired the lovely and popular Viola Brooke. I thought—I thought we were in love. I discovered eventually that Aubrey loved no one but himself. When fame came to him after the war through his writing he didn't need me, and then the sadistic turning of the screws began." A hollow sound that might have been a laugh came out of the old woman's throat. "I could have destroyed him then, Chambrun, but I didn't because I thought I loved him. The things he did to humiliate and shame me are too painful to revive here. I was in the theatre, doing a play in the West End. It was a long run hit. A young man named Haven began to pay me attentions. I was used to that sort of thing. A great many people imagined they were in love with Viola Brooke. George Haven persisted. At some point I tried to be rid of him by telling him the whole miserable story of my relationship with Aubrey. It didn't turn him away. He was suddenly a safe port in a storm that was wrecking me. One night, just before a performance, he came to my dressing room. Did I say that he was an engineer for a big oil company? Just beginning—at the very bottom of the ladder. He told me he'd been ordered to the Middle East. He had told his employers he was married and had to take his wife. His ship was sailing at ten o'clock that night. He begged me to come with him. I said no, I couldn't. My play. My career. And then, when he had gone, I knew he was my one hope for any kind of life. I walked out of the theatre in the middle of a performance. I met him at the ship without any belongings. I never went back to my apartment for anything. We sailed. We were married by the captain. 'Viola Brooke' was a stage name. I was married under my own, my legal name. If some ship news reporter picked it up it meant nothing. Now I was Mrs. George Haven, which had no news value either.

"Our first post was in the desert. There were three

other white men at the post, engineers like George. None of them knew me by sight. We became a part of that world. An occasional newspaper from home told us of the furore my disappearance had created. But the stage photographs of Viola Brooke didn't ring any bells where we were. I knew how to change my appearance. And finally—well, as long as we stayed out of England, we were safe. We didn't want the story revived. We didn't want Aubrey to know. And so we lived for three decades in the Middle East. George was a wonderful, kindly man and I grew to love him deeply. And he was a success. At the end of thirty years he was a very rich man and I—I was a middle-aged and aging woman who bore not the slightest resemblance to Viola Brooke.

"It seemed safe enough to come back to England. It was then that I began to see the kind of life Aubrey had lived, the havoc he had created in other lives. It was a shocking discovery, Chambrun, because I could have prevented it."

"You keep saying that, Mrs. Haven. How?"

"Aubrey Moon's whole career is based on fraud," she said, quietly. "His first novel, *Battle Array*, which won him literary acclaim, sold to the movies, was dramatized—which made Aubrey Moon the brightest of all planets in the literary world—was not his."

"I beg your pardon?" Chambrun said, his voice startled.

"A young officer on leave in Paris gave Aubrey the manuscript of a novel to read. Before Aubrey could return the script with his comments the young officer was killed in action. Aubrey hung onto the script waiting for someone to claim it. No one came forward. Before the idea occurred to him of claiming the book as his own, Aubrey had given the script to me to read. So I knew. And when the book came out under Aubrey's name, I knew. Oh, there were a few changes. But it was not Aubrey's book. I was distressed, but I was in love, so I let it go by. And, ironically, it was the book and its success that separated us. Afterwards I didn't want anything but escape, which my dear George provided for me." Mrs. Haven paused to finish off her drink.

Finally she went on. "George died five years ago. England was too painful a place for me to live, and so I came to America. One day about a year ago Ozman Gamayel came to see me. Ozman was the one person in all our years in the Middle East who had recognized me. Like a good friend he had kept the secret because he, too, was a victim of Aubrey's—some political indiscretion. Ozman told me a pretty frightening story. Age had made Aubrey even more bitter, more cruel. There were a dozen stories of people suffering under his oppression. Ozman knew how Aubrey was prepared to pay off if anything happened to him. What could be done? What could be done to check Aubrey? Well, I thought I knew.

"I came here to the Beaumont to see him. I can't duplicate the scene for you, Chambrun. The Stewart girl was there and heard what followed. It may explain why he had to keep her from talking. Poor lost girl! A prize example of Aubrey's special screw-turning technique. She had been in love with a young man who went to fight in Korea. She'd been indiscreet. There was a child. The man was captured by the Chinese Reds and was one of those who turned traitor. She has been trying to bring up the child, keeping his illegitimacy and his father's history a secret. Aubrey knew and Aubrey dangled her like a fish on a hook."

The old woman was silent for a moment, her eyes closed.

"What happened when you faced Moon, Mrs. Haven?" Chambrun asked, gently.

"He began by laughing at me; at the caricature of myself I'd become. It was the wrong tack, because I was no longer woundable in this area. And so, Chambrun, I played my cards. He must put a stop to his insane sadism or I would make public the truth about his beginning. I thought he might kill me then and there where I sat. Fortunately, before going to see him, I had made a statement, signed and witnessed, about *Battle Array* and placed in a safety deposit box.

"It was a stalemate. I had played his own game against him. If he went on with his game I would reveal him. If I told the truth about him he would take his revenge on Ozman and the others. I know my man, Chambrun. At this late date, draped in laurel wreaths, he couldn't stand even the hint that his career was based on a literary theft. I bought my apartment here in the hotel, and I have lived next to him as a sort of watchdog. Until the Prym girl's suicide and the apparent existence of a plot against Aubrey, things have been relatively quiet. Then Ozman and I thought some one of the others, tried past endurance, was planning to kill Aubrey, come what may."

After a long silence, Chambrun said: "I'm afraid it's Moon who's been tried past endurance, Mrs. Haven."

Calls were coming less frequently to Mrs. Veach's desk. The blueprints in front of her were dotted with thumbtacks. The search for Moon had so far failed.

A decision had to be made about Mrs. Haven, and she wasn't easy to handle. She insisted on going back to her own apartment.

"You can protect me there," she told Hardy, "as well as anywhere else. Apparently Aubrey has left the hotel. If he comes back you can surely prevent his getting to me."

Short of a jail cell, Hardy told himself, she would be as safe there as anywhere else. They could cover the front hall and the service entrance. There'd be no way Moon could possibly get back up to the roof. They could take her up, search her apartment and the roof area outside her place, put a cordon around the pent-house and no one could get to her.

Chambrun seemed less at ease about it. "Let's be clear about one thing, Mrs. Haven. Moon must know by now that we're on to him. He knows that sooner or later we'll find him and he'll be charged with the Stewart girl's murder. Knowing the way his mind works he'll certainly make a desperate effort to get at you, the cause of all his trouble. After that he won't care what happens to him."

"How can he get at me?" Mrs. Haven asked. "Your men will be blocking all the ways to my apartment."

"I don't know," Chambrun said. "He knows you, Mrs. Haven, better than we do."

"He knew me forty years ago," she said, drily. "I'm not the same person."

Chambrun shook his head. "He knows you today. He knows you were willing to run some risks to stand between him and his sadistic fun. I'm worried about Mr. Gamayel. Suppose Moon called you and told you Gamayel's life depended on your making a rendezvous with him?"

The old woman stared at Chambrun hard. "What should I do?" she asked.

"Stay put. Nothing. Believe nothing," Chambrun said. "I'd like to make a suggestion. I'd like Miss Barnwell and Mr. Wills to stay in your apartment with you. I'd rather you were never alone for a minute. If Moon should telephone you I'd like Wills to talk to him, tell him he's had it. I don't want him playing on your sympathy for a friend." He shook his head. "I don't know what I expect, Mrs. Haven, but I'm afraid of something that none of us is foreseeing."

"I want to go," John said. "But not Alison. Leave her out of it. If there's a showdown I want to be in on it, Mrs. Haven, believe me."

Chambrun gave him an odd look. "I think Alison

185

would like to be in on it too, John. And I'd like a woman there with Mrs. Haven. Don't ask me why. I just want to be certain there's nothing we've overlooked."

Chambrun's anxiety seemed farfetched to John. Hardy and his men went up ahead to the apartment. They would search it and then telephone down. No one had been allowed to the roofs since Moon's disappearance. Once the phone call came an elevator would be waiting just outside Chambrun's office. The hallway would be kept clear and Mrs. Haven would then be taken right up to her own front door, surrounded every step of the way.

Old Mrs. Haven showed no signs of excitement. John, standing close to Alison, felt no such calm. Somehow he had been infected by Chambrun's anxiety. If Moon was ever going to strike it would have to be quickly, before the wall around Mrs. Haven was too high for him ever to scale.

The phone rang. It was Hardy from the Haven penthouse. The coast was clear. No sign of trouble.

Chambrun went out into the hall and rang for an elevator. When the car came he signaled to John who was in the doorway. Two cops walked down the hallway in opposite directions, ready for any sudden trouble. Then John and Alison quickly herded the old woman across the hall and into the elevator.

Hardy met them outside the door to the penthouse.

"It's all clear here, Mrs. Haven," he said, confidently.

The blast of warm air from inside the cluttered apartment greeted them as they went in. Alison stared around her, wide-eyed. Mrs. Haven was as unconcerned as if she were simply entertaining friends—until she turned to the little wicker basket where Toto normally held court.

"Silly boy," she said. "When he's put out with me

for being away too long, he always goes back and gets on my bed, which is against the rules."

She sailed across the living room and down the corridor toward her bedroom. John and Alison and Chambrun, fidgeting nervously with his cigarette lighter, waited for her to return. Hardy came in from the hall, having placed his men.

"Where is she?" he asked.

"Went to get her dog," Chambrun said.

They heard her booming voice. "Toto, you naughty boy, where are you?"

"There wasn't any dog in here," Hardy said. "I covered every inch of the place."

Chambrun stared at Hardy—and then, far away, they heard a wail of distress. Toto was in some kind of trouble.

"Come on!" Chambrun said.

John was directly behind the hotel manager as they hurried down the corridor. A gust of cold night air swept past them. A window was open somewhere, John thought. Toto's wail was clearer, but still far away.

"The blasted dog has got out on the roof!" Chambrun said. "Mrs. Haven!" he called loudly. "We'll get him for you!"

At the end of the hall was a door to Mrs. Haven's section of the roof. It was open. As Chambrun and John reached it they saw the old woman, her evening wrap fluttering in the wind, opening a gate which opened into the next section of roof.

"Toto!" they heard her call over the wind.

John sprinted past Chambrun to get to her, just as she stepped through the gate. He found himself frozen as he came up behind her. The next section of roof was, he suddenly realized, Moon's.

Mrs. Haven had stopped just in front of him, her fox-lined wrap billowing out behind her like wings. A few yards in front of her, wriggling desperately on the tarred floor of the roof, was Toto. His front and hind feet had been tied together so that he couldn't move. He cried out piteously at the sight of the old woman.

Standing just beyond the dog, framed by two huge evergreens growing in tubs, was Aubrey Moon. He was hatless and coatless, his thin hair whipping around in the wind.

"You malicious old bitch!" John heard him say. "So you finally caught up with me in the end. But there's a price attached to it, Viola. A very high price."

He raised his right hand and pointed his gun directly at Mrs. Haven's broad bosom.

John shouted at the top of his lungs hoping to distract Moon's attention. At the same moment a shadowy figure rose up from behind one of the evergreens. There was a slashing movement and Moon screamed. The gun dropped to the floor of the roof. John dove for it and fell on top of it. Absurdly enough he heard Mrs. Haven saying: "Poor Toto. My dearest Toto. Hasn't anyone got a knife?"

John was on his feet. Moon was crazily flailing at the man who'd attacked him. His right arm hung useless at his side. The other man struck again and Moon went down and lay still.

Chambrun and Hardy, the latter with a flashlight, were behind them now and John saw Mr. Ozman Gamayel wiping off the silver head of his black Malacca walking stick with a handkerchief. He ignored John and walked quietly past him to Mrs. Haven, who was cradling Toto in her arms.

"My dear Viola, what have I done?" he cried, in a distressed voice. "I crept up here to protect him when I heard about the Stewart girl. And now I've done the very thing we feared. But when I saw him point that gun at you—"

"Don't be an idiot, Ozman," the old lady boomed. "You're suddenly a hero. Do you, by any chance have a penknife? He's trussed up poor Toto like a Thanksgiving turkey."

Moon was not badly hurt, the police doctor reported. It wasn't hard to figure what had happened. Without questioning Moon it was partial guesswork, but sound enough. Somehow he knew that Chambrun had guessed the truth. Perhaps, on his trips down from the penthouse he had returned to Alison's office and overheard. After that he had only one aim. Mrs. Haven must be punished, and it no longer mattered whether he got away with it or not. But how? She would be watched, the roof covered. So he'd slipped back up the service stair and surprised Hardy's man Palmer. Instead of escaping down through the hotel he'd gone up the next service stairway to Mrs. Haven's back door. He'd waited there until Hardy finally withdrew his men from the roof to aid in the search of the hotel. He had the passkey he had taken from Margo Stewart. That he had killed Margo was certain. She had known about Mrs. Haven. She knew or guessed the truth about the supposed plan to kill Moon. Moon himself was responsible. Perhaps, half-tight, she threatened him with it. He had followed her to John's room and killed her, being fairly certain John would be blamed for it.

"So he waited outside Mrs. Haven's place until I had cleared the roof," Hardy said. "He let himself in her back door with the passkey. Fortunately she wasn't there. She'd gone to the opera."

They were gathered in the old woman's living room, all gratefully sampling her Kentucky corn whiskey. All, that is, except Gamayel who toyed with his peach-colored liqueur in the tapered glass.

"It was safe for him to go back to his own apartment then," Hardy went on. "We wouldn't look for him there again. We never did search the penthouse level until we prepared to bring Mrs. Haven up here. So he figured out a plan. He came back in here and took the dog. He knew she'd come running the minute she heard the dog's cry of distress. She'd be an open target, no matter who was behind to protect her. But for Mr. Gamayel he would have succeeded."

"And I," Gamayel said, "was cursing myself for an idiot. I knew nothing of the new turn of events. I went for a walk. I was troubled. I felt, somehow, the man plotting against Aubrey would strike when he could. Over the rooftops was the obvious way to get at Aubrey. I wondered how carefully the roof was being watched. I came back to the hotel. I made no effort to hide my return. I suspect it was at the precise moment when excitement was at its highest. The plain fact of it is, no one noticed me. I went through the passage to the service elevator which is self-operated at night. I went up to the roof. As simple as that."

"You can build a ten-foot wall around a place and someone always manages to find a loose brick," Hardy said.

"I was snooping around on the roof, alarmed to find none of your men there Hardy. Alarmed at the simplicity with which I'd got there myself. I was about to come downstairs and remonstrate with you when I saw a light go on and then off in Mrs. Haven's apartment. I knew she was at the opera. She would never miss a performance by Nilsson. So I hid behind one of the evergreen bushes to see what would happen. You can imagine my surprise when I saw Aubrey come out of your apartment, my dear, carrying Toto." He shrugged. "I was puzzled by the police searching your apartment a little later. Then, a moment after they'd gone, Aubrey appeared with Toto, trussed up the way he was, and put him down on the roof. The poor little fellow cried inconsolably. And then—well, you came for him. My actions were instinctive."

Mrs. Haven rocked Toto gently in her lap. "I think

we have won the day, Ozman," she said. "Aubrey will be tried for murder—murder of the Stewart girl. He will not use the evidence against our friends, because I will not make public the story of *Battle Array*. He will pay any price, I think, to preserve his literary immortality." She beamed at John and Alison and the others. "It seems that at last our cannibal has overeaten. Fill up the glasses, Wills, I'd like to drink to that."